Last Sermon for a Sinner

Claremary P. Sweeney

Publisher's Information
EBookBakery Books

Author contact: claremarypsweeney@yahoo.com
Author website: https://claremarypsweeney.carrd.co
Author blog: AroundZuZusBarn.com

Cover and map design by Zachary Perry

ISBN 978-1-938517-93-8

1. Mystery. 2. Claremary P. Sweeney 3. South County, RI. 4. Peace Dale, RI. 5. Easter Season 6. Women Sleuths. 7. Murder.

© 2019 by Claremary P. Sweeney

For Charley
who taught me to look at orange flowers in a kinder, gentler light

and

for all those we forever carry in our hearts

PEACE DALE, RHODE ISLAND

HAZARD MEMORIAL BUILDING (1902)
WITH FOUNTAIN

There are a hundred places where I fear
To go - so with his memory they brim.
And entering with relief some quiet place
Where never fell his foot or shone his face
I say, "There is no memory of him here!"
And so stand stricken, so remembering him.

from "Time Does Not Bring Relief" *(Sonnet II)*
Edna St. Vincent Millay

SUMMERTIME PAST

Marjorie Tucker heard the ice cream truck's jingle coming from the next street. The driver had stopped going by her house the day the posters with the picture of her son were being hung on telephone poles and in storefront windows throughout the town – the morning after Anthony had disappeared.

During those humid summer weeks, neighbors visited the house with food and words of comfort she barely heard and now couldn't recall. But she vividly remembered the events of that terrible day. Sometimes memories of it engulfed her whole consciousness, playing over and over again. Never-ending nightmares.

That July afternoon, six years ago, she hadn't realized how late it was until the truck was right outside the front door. As usual, the driver waited for Anthony to come running down the stairs to proudly offer his piggy bank coins for an orange creamsicle. Most of the kids in the neighborhood wanted fudgicles or cherry popsicles or chocolate ice cream cones. But Anthony loved the color orange. "Like my hair, Mommy," he would tell her, holding the treat close to his face, the cool ice cream brushing against the wisps of soft ringlets falling into his eyes.

Once, when they were shopping at Belmont's, she stopped the cart by the freezer and reached in to get a box of his favorite frozen treat.

"No, Mommy. I only like the kind from the ice cream truck," he told her.

She'd put the package back even though it was the exact same brand he sat eating every day in the summer on their front stoop while the sound of the truck's jingle faded into the distance.

Marjorie hadn't noticed the time passing. She'd been busy doing a wash. Dusting. Baking cookies. Visiting with a neighbor. Changing the linens on the beds. Phoning to make a doctor's appointment for Anthony's annual check-up. Trying to get a plumber out to fix a leaking faucet. Waiting on hold. Listening to Muzak. Precious minutes lost.

Her son had gone off to summer Bible school and never returned to her. Saint Bibiana's was only a few blocks away. Sometimes she met him there in the afternoon and they would walk home together. He loved to stop and ask the names of the orange flowers in the gardens along the way. He'd wait patiently by the trumpet vine twining around the church's signpost until a hummingbird fluttered along hovering for a sip of nectar. That day, Anthony rode home on the bus with his friends - and then vanished into thin air. That summer, the air was thick and heavy. She remembered sweat mingled with tears.

Often she thought she heard his voice calling. The sound of his laughter. She felt him close to her, still. Nearby – but where?

She knew the ice cream man was being kind, but the melody from a truck Marjorie couldn't see broke her heart anew every day.

Last Sermon for a Sinner

MARCH

*March, master of winds, bright minstrel and marshal
of storms that enkindle the season they smite.*

from "March: An Ode"
Algernon Charles Swinburne

The Ides of March are come

from *Julius Caesar (Act III Scene 1)*
William Shakespeare

Friday, March 16

G ilbert Cheevers stared up at the arched wooden beams. It was the Ides of March –or close enough. A storm was brewing outside the stained glass windows of the church. He could feel a chill in his bones and wondered what ill wind would blow into the sanctuary that night. Confessions at Saint Bibiana's wouldn't be starting for at least two hours.

He enjoyed having the church to himself. Lying in the pew with his head propped up on a couple of hymnals; he peeled the wrapper from the sandwich he'd found in the refrigerator in the pantry. Much to his disappointment, his wife, Darlene, couldn't abide the smell of any kind of fish in the house. He sniffed deeply. Ah, tuna salad! And it was still fresh! In his estimation, this was always the best day around the church because some Catholics still refrained from eating meat on Friday during Lent - obeying an edict long stricken from the rulebooks. *My soul for a tuna sandwich!* He chuckled to himself, taking a bite and savoring the taste before washing it down with a swig of milk.

Gilbert had his own home - his own kitchen, his own refrigerator, his own couch, and his own bed. He even had a private man cave in his cellar. It wasn't much - an old, brown, corduroy Barcalounger recliner a neighbor had put out on the sidewalk on trash day; a General Electric television set which pulled in a couple of channels; a beat-up transistor radio for listening to the Red Sox games; a five-piece set of rusted metal tray tables he got for free at the Jonnycake Center to put his stuff on; a mini fridge stocked with beer. There was a folding chair on the other side of the trays. In case anyone came to visit. Nobody ever did. It was a good thing, he told himself. He had the place all to himself and he liked it like that. The cave was his refuge - his escape from Darlene and her merry band of biddies.

During the past few years, the women had begun taking over his house. Doreen, Cheryl, and Annette. He often wondered if it was a coincidence or if Darlene had picked her friends solely on the basis of their names, which were the same as the girls in the original Mickey Mouse Club from back in the Fifties. The Four Mouseketeers they called themselves.

It wasn't so bad at first. Cheryl and Doreen were tolerable and he actually had taken a shining to Annette. She always showed up with goodies. His favorite were the Tollhouse Cookies like the ones his mother baked every Saturday afternoon when he was younger. Soft and sweet and gooey. Annette must have taken them out of the oven right before she came to the house. They were still warm when she brought them in on two china blue plates. The smaller one she presented to him. When Annette smiled at Gilbert, he got lost in those big brown eyes - like luscious, milk chocolate Hershey Kisses. He could have melted right there in front of her.

Eventually, the Four Mouseketeers dwindled to three. They'd all gone line dancing one Saturday night at the Elks Club and Annette found herself a beau – a dorky, rich guy who kept a boat docked down at Hanson's Landing. She took up sailing and the smell of freshly baked cookies in the Cheevers' house became a thing of the past.

It wasn't long until Darlene replaced her with Minnie Jacques. He was certain Minnie was a nickname Darlene had bestowed on her so she'd fit in better with the group. It didn't matter. Gilbert had his own nickname for her – Tiny Jackass. The day she showed up at their house marked when things began going downhill for Gilbert. He came into the living room one morning and there she was, sacked out, feet barely reaching to the opposite end of the chintz-covered love seat. He stood staring down at her face. It was the color of putty. Its pock-mocked craters were filled with dried makeup reminding him of the Spackle he used to plug in the nail holes Darlene kept banging in the walls for pictures she never seemed to get around to hanging.

The dwarf on the sofa had bleached blond hair cut in a bob like the little Dutch Boy's on the almost empty paint cans in the garage. She was wearing a black and red polka dotted skirt, a frilly white blouse, and yellow knee socks. He wondered out loud to Darlene if she'd bought the outfit in the children's section of Kenyon's Department Store. His wife haughtily informed him Minnie had her own personal shopper and purchased all her designer clothes at the trendiest stores and boutiques.

"Boooteeks? Well, laaadeedaaa!" Gilbert wasn't impressed. No matter what that woman wore, she reminded him of the cupie doll his father had won at a booth in the Crescent Park Amusement Center when he was a little tyke. It was so long ago; he couldn't recall the exact year. But he did remember sitting on his bed yanking out all the doll's pink feathers, leaving just a shiny, squat, plastic body filled with teeny holes. If he held the doll up to a lamp, light would shine through its hollow, little body. He'd love to yank out Minnie's feathers.

For a brief moment, Gilbert pictured Tiny Jackass naked, her skin riddled with pockmarks even Spackle couldn't fix. He balled up his fists, rubbing at his closed eyelids to erase the sight. He knew from the start he was destined to loathe this woman and in the months following, his premonition came true. *Soooo much not to like.*

In Gilbert's estimation, the worst thing about Minnie wasn't her priggishness. It was the fact she couldn't hold her liquor. After two drinks she'd be slurring her words, putting a "y" on the end of everyone's name - Darleney, Doreeny, Sherry, Gilbey. He despised being called Gilbey.

When he politely requested she refrain from using nicknames and call him Gilbert, she grabbed at his sleeve acting all slobbery like she was his best friend. "Oh, Gilbey, wookit yaw ittle wed cheeks. How cute ooo is."

And Doreeny, Darleeney, and Sherry laughed and agreed with her assessment that he was "the most adawable widdle Gilbey on earth."

Some nights, after she'd slid under the dining room table, they'd call on him to help. He would be summoned up from the cellar to haul her dead weight to the sofa so she could sleep it off.

Once, he'd complained about this to Darlene and she scolded him.

"You'd get drunk too, if you had to go home to that husband of hers."

He'd met the husband on a few occasions. The poor man hadn't struck Gilbert as being all that bad. Professor Maxwell Jacques, once a man of stature, was now pale, wrinkled, and bent over. The first time they'd met, Gilbert remembered him holding out a dry, limp hand to shake. His fleeting smile revealed crooked, yellowed teeth. The old boy sat in a rocking chair the whole evening never uttering a single word. Darlene commented he could have been one of the needlepoint throw pillows for all the conversation he offered. It occurred to Gilbert what with Tiny Jackass's constant chatter and tee-heeing, Maxwell had given up trying to get a word in edgewise years ago.

The Mouseketeers loved to get together and talk. Sometimes they all spoke in unison, their high-pitched voices bouncing off the kitchen walls. Like a flock of seagulls, they were. A murder of crows, he thought. Four inane conversations about drivel, overlapped with high-pitched squeals and frequent breaks for chugging their drinks.

Most days they were out and about - shopping, bowling, power walking the paths around the nearby graveyard, lying on the beach in the summer. When the weather wasn't cooperative, they parked their butts in his living room, knitting needles and false teeth clacking away. Other times they sat nattering around the dining room table, coloring or playing cards, dominoes or mah-jongg. One of them always seemed to be holding court on the throne in the bathroom whenever he most needed to use it. And when they weren't freeloading at his house, the pungent stench of their cheap perfumes and hairsprays lingered, permeating the air around him.

He made it a point always to be polite and not let them know what was roiling inside. His mother had instilled good manners into his character from a young age. She came from class; a proud descendent of the Hazard Family who built Peace Dale up from a handful of households to the village it was today.

Needless to say, there were times when his man cave wasn't far enough away from the women's incessant chatter. Times when he preferred being elsewhere. Tucked inside the hip pocket of his moth-eaten, woolen sweater vest was the spare church key. He'd made a copy from the one he'd pilfered months ago from the secretary's desk drawer in the office to use whenever he needed a short vacation away from his wife. He loved Darlene with his whole heart and soul, but forty-two years with any one woman could wear a man down. And she'd never been easy to live with.

He took another bite, smacking his lips at the hint of celery salt he detected. The bread was soft and white. It brought him back to his childhood and he smiled as he thought about Wonder Bread. Darlene often bragged to the girls that her husband's best attribute was the fact it didn't take much to make him happy. Gilbert couldn't disagree with her. Life was good and he intended to grab as much joy from each passing day as he could.

A brisk wind blew in from the back of the church and hovered over the pew. A creaking sound jolted him from his reverie. Someone was entering the confessional. Father Erlich wasn't due until two minutes to seven. Gilbert knew the priest's habits well and the man was nothing, if not predictable and prompt.

"Bless me, Father, for I have sinned."

He didn't recognize the speaker. Gilbert was familiar with Erlich's monotonous, mumbling recitations and this definitely wasn't the pastor's voice.

"It's been six years since my last confession …"

Well then, six years, huh? I guess this could take a while. Gilbert scootched himself down closer to the end of the bench nearest the confessional booth to listen in. He could understand why someone who'd been accumulating sins for so many years would need a practice session alone before the priest arrived.

Gilbert made it a point to confess his own sins each week. He was always the last person in the confessional every Friday night. His memory was lapsing lately and he didn't want a forgotten venial transgression to send him plummeting into the raging fires of purgatory at the moment of his death.

In religion class, he'd been taught it took indulgences to get you out. He remembered the prayer cards of his youth. His missal, the one his aunt had given him for First Communion, was filled with holy cards he'd collected. His favorite one was of the poor, tortured souls waste-deep in the flames, arms imploringly stretched above their heads toward heaven waiting to be freed from the endless sea of lapping orange tongues of fire. Gilbert was pretty sure, when he died, few would remember to say a Hail Mary for his smoldering soul let alone give a monetary donation for his eternal salvation. *But at least I've got half a chance. Not like those poor, little, unchristened babies left over in Limbo before that rule was changed.*

A strangled sob from the confessional brought Gilbert into the present. The penitent's soul-searching became even fainter. He couldn't tell if it was a man or woman. Gilbert detected only a few of the words.

"... accident ... stopped breathing ... body ... forgiveness ... please ...."

Gilbert strained to hear but the muffled voice had begun to pray, ebbing and flowing into the softest whisper.

"Hail Mary ... grace ... blessed art ... pray for us sinners ... hour of our death, Amen."

Creaks and then footsteps echoed in the church. An icy draft traveled swiftly down the marble tiles of the center aisle and the front door slammed shut. Gilbert cautiously poked his head up over the back of the pew, stifling the urge to give chase and call out, "Hey! It doesn't count. You have to get absolution." But the sinner was long gone. Gilbert picked up the milk carton to return it to the refrigerator in the kitchen and see what he could find for dessert.

❧

6:53 PM chimed from the mantelpiece clock. Father Erlich finished his cold, instant butterscotch pudding leaving the film of brownish yellow skin in the bottom of the bowl. He looked up at the clock on the kitchen wall and then down at the uneaten food on his plate. Rising from his seat at the table, he walked to the sink and stuffed the fish cakes, Brussels sprouts, and boiled potatoes into the garbage disposal. If Mrs. Brody knew he was wasting food every night, food the starving little children in Africa, who she sent money to each month, would be thankful for, she'd have a fit. She wasn't the greatest cook, although, she did keep a clean house - immaculate he thought. But the dinners she left warming in the oven for him each evening were colorless and bland. It really didn't matter. He'd had no appetite for anything lately.

The old priest liked to spend his mealtime in silence and so, most evenings, Father Lucien ate earlier with Mrs. Brody. After she'd left for home, the younger priest made himself scarce when Erlich came into the kitchen.

Often, Lucien would be invited to a parishioner's house for dinner, but no one ever extended the invitation to Father Erlich, having found out during the first years of his assignment to the parish their pastor was not exactly the sociable type. He didn't seem to like people. While other priests and pastors could be seen after Sunday services on the front steps greeting churchgoers, Erlich left hastily through the back door, returning to the rectory before the smoke from the altar candles had dissipated. It was said, among his parishioners, he had an aversion to germs and didn't like to shake hands. Truth be told, most weren't too eager to touch him either.

Erlich was tolerated by the members of his flock and many agreed, although his sermons were boring and went off on endless nonsensical tangents, he did his job relatively well. He heard confessions, distributed Holy Communion, said Masses on Sundays and holy days and he was at his best when called upon to give the Last Rites and officiate at a funeral. He was comfortable around death. Anything else parishioners needed in order to save their souls was taken care of by the youthful, more popular priest whom they all liked. They secretly longed for the day when Father Lucien would become the pastor. But he seemed in no hurry to take over and had settled comfortably into his own routine around the parish.

Total opposites, they were. Father Yin and Father Yang, the two were nicknamed early on. The relationship worked fine for everyone involved.

Erlich flipped on the outside floodlight. Not many cars were in the lot as he strolled toward the church. He came in the front door and walked slowly down the side aisle to the confessional booth. A few old women, their heads wrapped in frayed, faded rayon kerchiefs tied securely under their chins, were scattered among the pews in the back of the Sanctuary.

The scarce number of penitents was a reminder to him that telling one's sins to a priest had gone out of vogue. He blamed the Protestants with their corporate confessions. Those people were way too free and easy with their forgiveness in his estimation. And for good measure, he put the onus squarely on this Pope who appeared to be launching his own private campaign to get rid of the age-old sins of the past. He'd even declared publicly atheists could get into heaven. *What was the man thinking? Atheists! If it were up to His Holiness, hell would go hurtling out of business in a handbag.* The old priest sat in the box fuming to himself as he waited for the night's first customer to come forward.

❦

2

Saturday, March 17

"Stinky, stinky, stinky, stinky." Connor ran from the kitchen holding his nose. The three-year-old crawled under the tent his brother had made for him of blankets and towels hung with clothespins between the chair and the couch.

Detective Carl Sullivan had just walked into the house, "What's the matter with your brother?" he asked Billy who was reading at the kitchen table.

"Connor apparently doesn't like the smell of corned beef and cabbage," his elder son said, not looking up from his book.

"What kind of Irish kid are we raising? And how did Max end up with my leprechaun sock on his tail?" He grabbed for the dog as it deftly dodged and ran from the room, disappearing under the tent. "I was looking for that this morning. I hate it when my socks don't match my tie." He kissed his wife who was standing at the stove stirring a large stock pot and tossed his jacket over the back of a chair before sitting down.

"Yes, I'll bet everybody at the station noticed your glaring fashion faux pas," she commented. "It must have been a torture for you today."

"STINKY!" came a voice from underneath the tent.

"Ask me how my morning was," his wife challenged him with a smirk.

"I think I can guess," he said. "Well if it's any consolation, I look forward to Saint Paddy's Day all year. I love your corned beef and cabbage."

"And then there's the corned beef sandwiches and the corned beef hash we get to eat for the next two weeks." Billy sarcastically threw his two cents into the conversation.

"And the corned beef cupcakes and the cabbage pie and the corned beef fudge," his father teased.

"Yuckey, yuckey, yuckey, yuckey!" Connor added in his own two cents from under the tent.

"How did everything go at work?" Jess brought him a plate of food ignoring the voice in the next room.

"We managed to get all of the final paperwork on the robbery case done early and in time for everyone to head out to the annual No Green Beer Here Celebration at the Sons of Liberty in Peace Dale. It was beginning to get a bit rowdy, so I decided to retreat to the peace and quiet of my loving family."

"Stinky, yuckey, stinky. Stinky, yuckey, stinky. Stinky, yuckey, stinky, Stinky, yuckey, stinky ..." The serenade coming from beneath the blanket faded in and out.

Billy stared at his father. "Peace and quiet? How many beers did you have?"

"Obviously not nearly enough. I'm thinking seriously of going back." Sullivan informed his son as the dog ran into the kitchen tripping over the green and gold striped scarf now wrapped around its neck.

Saturday Bible School at Saint Bibiana's was over. The children had been loaded onto the bus, the shamrock cards they'd made for their parents carefully tucked into backpacks. They settled into seats for the short ride through the nearby neighborhoods. Miss Laura was gathering stray crayons and green construction paper from the last project of the day when she heard a thud. She looked up, tilting her head to one side and stopping to listen closely. Only silence came from the church office rooms above.

"The tables are cleaned and I put them away in the back of the store room. I'd stay to help you, but I've got an early play rehearsal at

the library. The crazy director blows a gasket if anyone comes in late."
Clovis grabbed his notebook and jacket from the closet. "Thanks, and
I'll see you next week."

Laura hardly had time to say, "No problem" before he was out
the door. She stood alone for a moment, in the middle of the room.
It always felt eerily quiet to her when the place wasn't filled with
laughing children. She took down the shamrocks, the leprechauns,
and the rainbows with their pots of gold, storing them in a carton
labeled St. Paddy's Day to be brought out the next year. From another
box she removed Easter decorations to be hung in the display case
along the back wall. She looked at the clock and decided to finish this
on Monday morning. It was getting late and she was looking forward
to the Guinness beef stew simmering in the slow cooker since early
morning.

She made sure the dehumidifier was emptied and the garbage was
securely tied up. She locked the door and walked to her car, stopping
to toss the bag into the dumpster at the edge of the parking lot. Lights
were out in the church office, which was not unusual for late Saturday
afternoon. Laura found it odd Father Erlich hadn't come by at the end
of the day. He often looked in on her after he'd finished practicing the
sermon for Sunday, cautioning her to drive safely, although she only
lived a mile away in a neighborhood known as The Oaks.

"Most accidents happen close to home," he never failed to remind
her.

"That's probably because of all the old geezers in this town like
you who should have had their licenses taken away years ago," Clovis
had mumbled under his breath after the pastor was safely out of
earshot. She'd given her young assistant a warning look, having been
brought up to respect priests and nuns and never to question them.
But she knew there was definitely some truth in what Clovis had
muttered.

The curtain moved slightly in the front window of the rectory.
Laura couldn't see who it was but she waved and drove off as the

lace fell back into place and a shade was drawn against the impending darkness.

༜

Clovis hid behind the curtains in the wings of the Peace Dale Library as the foppish little man center stage ranted and raved.

"Is this town totally devoid of talent? You call what you're doing acting?" Ishmael Hitchcock screamed. He flung his black velvet beret like a Frisbee at the young woman playing Mollie, causing her to cry out in surprise.

The rehearsal was a complete disaster. Some of the cast still had not memorized their lines and the director was on a tear.

"This isn't Shakespeare, people! The last time I checked, there were no fools in any of the scenes. Maybe that's what we need? A play filled with village idiots. Somebody find me a play about village idiots so I can typecast this bunch of wannabe thespians."

Sophia Carnavale was observing from the back of the room. She'd been on the Board of Directors for the Peace Dale Community Players for three years. They agreed they'd never dealt with a director as temperamental as Ishmael Hitchcock. People were leaving the show in droves. Most of the stage crew had quit and now, she watched in horror as the actor playing Mr. Paravicini threw down his script and stormed out. Something had to be done and fast. Luckily the publicity had not been sent out and the scheduled performance on the first weekend in April could be moved to a later time, if necessary. She made her decision and walked determinedly to the front of the hall.

"Mr. Hitchcock, could I interrupt your little tirade to speak with you in private?"

The director swung around to glare at her from the stage. "Excuse me? Tirade? Exactly what is the subtext I'm to take from your words?" He stomped down the stairs to pose irately in front of her.

She towered over the man and bent forward to look him straight in the eyes. "Tirade, harangue, diatribe, tantrum, hissy fit. Read into it what you like but the bottom line is, you're fired!"

Sighs of relief and a few nervous giggles caused the ex-director to point his cane at the troupe who'd clustered together on the stage. Swirling the satin cape around his shoulders, he informed her, "You can't fire me. I quit!" He charged from the room only to return and hurl one last insult before leaving. "Unsophisticated, illiterate yokels!"

An emergency meeting was called. Sophia shook her head and looked at the other members of the board as she finished explaining what had happened at rehearsal. "I never liked that guy. He's been verbally abusive to the cast and crew. It's a wonder they're not all suffering from post-traumatic stress syndrome. He's lucky I didn't call the cops."

"We agree you did the right thing but I've already paid him most of the money in the budget for this production," the treasurer announced. "I guess we'll have to cancel it."

"Not so fast. I think I have a way of making sure the show still goes on. My friends owe me big time. I'm positive if I ask them nicely, they'll do it for free," Sophia announced confidently to those present.

On her way home in the car, she phoned her sister-in-law, Ruth Eddleman Carnavale, pleading her case. "You teach English. This is a famous English play. You love mysteries. This is a famous English mystery. And you've directed one-acts for the college competition. I can sew costumes; Rick and Gino could finish painting the set and help with the lighting. Samuel can assist Clovis, our stage-manager. Arthur and Clay will take care of finding set pieces and props. This will be fun," she declared. Ruth had her doubts.

During the next hour, Sophia made more calls and even convinced her best friend, Kara Langley, to be the assistant director in spite of her reluctance.

"I've never had anything to do with any kind of stage production in my entire life," she said. "And besides, I'm back to working part time on the police force and at the forensics lab."

"And I work full time at the hospital and do extra shifts when needed. What's your point? This will only be two nights a week until the middle of April. You can help Ruth. Be her right-hand person. Run lines with the cast; give the actors their cues; tell everyone how great they're doing," Sophia cajoled. "Besides, Ruth is going to cast Stewart as Mr. Paravicini. If you want to see your husband at all for the next month, you'll agree to be at rehearsals. And he'll need your help getting into character. Be the cheerleader. I'm sure you can handle that."

"Rah, rah," she said resignedly. When Sophia made up her mind, Kara knew nothing could change it.

Stewart Langley was overjoyed at his newly found avocation, especially since his character spoke with an Italian accent. He loved doing accents, much to his wife's dismay. John Wayne, Maurice Chevalier, Inspector Clouseau, Bob Cratchit, Jerry Lewis, Pepe le Pew - all were part of his repertoire. He was a brilliant scientist and a marvelous teacher, but in her opinion, linguistics was definitely not his forte.

Sophia's husband, Gino, wasn't pleased. He felt the part of Paravicini was made for him and complained to his wife that Ruth was biased in choosing Stewart because they'd been friends longer. "He don't even talk right, Sophia. Who speaks betta eyetalian den me? Dat accent he's usin ain't even close to eyetalian!"

Sophia assured him this was not the case. "Ruth knows you'll be more valuable creating the set design. And you'll get to spend time with Rick. You love working with your brother."

Gino had been a window dresser in New York City before moving to Rhode Island, and he welcomed any opportunity to use his talents to create imaginative scenes. As the head custodian at the Washington County Courthouse Center for the Arts, he was kept busy taking care of the historic building and making backdrops and sets for many of the plays and concerts presented there. His twin brother, Rick, was an art teacher at the university and Gino looked to him for advice on all his projects. It would be a chance for them to work together and Sophia knew this would appease him for not getting cast as Paravicini in the play.

At the end of the night, Sophia sat back, put her hands behind her head and feet up, congratulating herself on a job well done. "Looks like the show will go on," she said to her husband, who was scanning the script.

"And if anythin' happens to Stewart, sos he can't do his part, I can be his stand-in. I already know all a my lines," Gino declared.

∼

Gilbert could hear them from his Barcalounger. In his hasty retreat down to the man cave, he hadn't shut the cellar door.

"So, what should we do tonight, ladies?" Darlene put veggie chips and avocado dip in the middle of the kitchen table.

"It's St. Patrick's Day. We could listen to Irish bands at the Pump House or walk down to the Elks Club and see if we can get lucky," Cheryl suggested. They all burst out laughing.

"You already hit the pot of gold. You're not married," Minnie stated, causing them to hoot louder and bang on the table.

"I'm not dressed for dancing. Besides, it's windy out there and it's going to rain. I can feel it in my bones. I'd rather hang around here drinking Bailey's and playing cards." Doreen double dipped a chip in the bowl causing Cheryl to make a pouty face.

"I got a new Mexican Train domino game. I could pop home and get it. When you press the button it goes wooooo,wooooo, chugga, chugga, chugga, chugga - real loud. It scared the crap out of Maxwell the other night when I tested it." Tiny Jackass placed her hand over her mouth and tee-heed.

"He's old as dirt. You could have given him a heart attack," Darlene said.

"I wish!" she retorted, causing them all to break out into high pitched, chalkboard scratching laughter. Minnie moved next to the open door. "Let's order a pizza and maybe we can coax Gilbert to come out of the cellar with some of that whiskey he likes to nip. He could entertain us by sharing a few of the sins he heard in church last night," she taunted loudly enough for him to hear.

Down in the man cave, Gilbert's face reddened. He jumped up and went to the foot of the stairs. He was livid. He'd confided in Darlene and she'd betrayed his confidence. Good he hadn't gone into any detail about what he'd actually heard. He couldn't believe she blabbed to those idiots. Now it would be all over the church by tomorrow morning. This was the last straw! He grabbed his jacket and cap, leaving by the bulkhead, furious with his wife and her band of old biddies. He heard the cackling coming from the open window above the sink all the way to the sidewalk as he escaped to Saint Bib's.

The church was lit up like an amusement park and police cars were in the lot when Gilbert arrived. People waited in groups on the sidewalk. He recognized some of his neighbors and joined them to gawk at the front doors of the building.

"What's going on?" he asked to no one in particular.

"Not sure, yet," a woman wearing a yellow plastic raincoat, sporting pink brush curlers tucked under a brown and black paisley kerchief answered. "The police have been in there for an hour."

"We can rule out someone being sick or hurt. They would have already called a rescue."

He recognized the speaker, Maxwell Jacques, and moved to stand beside him.

"Gilbert Cheevers," he held out his hand and when Jacques gave him a blank stare, he attempted to jar the old man's memory. "My wife, Darlene, is friends with your wife Minnie." Jacques continued to gape. "We've met a few times. We live on the corner of Austin and High. Your wife and my wife are friends. She spends a lot of time at my place," Gilbert explained.

"Lucky you," Jacques finally responded with a hint of sarcasm in his voice.

Gilbert found himself warming up to this man. He offered a start to the conversation. "I heard you retired from the university."

"That was a couple of years ago. I wanted to stay but it seems they were intent on adding some new blood to the engineering department," he said.

"So, what do you do to keep yourself busy?"

"I volunteer at the Senior Center, fixing things and I run the sound system for all the productions at the library. Sometimes I get called to do some work at the church. I putter around my yard, teach a class or two at the Peace Dale Guild.

"My mom used to bring me to the Guild when I was a kid. She took sewing lessons there," Gilbert was beginning to feel nostalgic. "She made all my clothes."

"They don't build places like that any more." Maxwell declared, "I've been reading up on the local architecture. Lots of history in this little village. The Guild dates back to 1908 when Augusta Hazard gave it as a gift to the village. Imagine giving a gift like that?"

"There wouldn't be a village without the Hazard family. They built the library, the stone mills, the old office building where the mill workers once lived. There's a museum of art and culture on the top floor filled with artifacts Rowland Hazard II collected from around the world."

"I visit there sometimes between classes," Maxwell said.

"My mother's great aunt was married to a Hazard. She was always quite proud of her origins. She had a lovely, cashmere shawl made in their textiles factory. Darlene wanted Mother to leave the shawl to her when she died, but she chose to be buried in it. Those two never got along well. Mother felt I'd married down."

They were distracted by the police leaving from the side door and getting into their vehicles. The lights went out. Father Lucien appeared on the steps. When the last car drove off, he came down to speak with the people congregating on the sidewalk. The woman in the curlers stepped forward. "Is everything okay, Father?"

"Yes, it appears there's been a break-in, but the police are investigating and I'm sure everything will be taken care of in due time. I hope to see you all in church tomorrow morning. I've got to go in and write a sermon now." He patted some of them on the back as they dispersed leaving only Gilbert and Maxwell standing together in the drizzle.

"Well, that's a bit unusual," Jacques mumbled to himself.

"What is?"

"Lucien giving the sermon. Erlich never lets him speak from the pulpit. I think the old guy's afraid he'll be upstaged and we'll start expecting more from his preaching in the future. The few times a year I do go to church, I appreciate the pastor's sermons. They allow me ample time to nap between the Gospel and Communion." Jacques turned to leave. "Well, I guess I'll see you around."

He began a slow shuffle along the sidewalk then suddenly turned. "Would you like to come to my place for a little nip? I live around the corner and down the bike path. It's Saint Paddy's Day and I got a really good bottle of whiskey when I was at The Sons of Liberty today. I haven't cracked it open yet. Just waiting for the right company to share it with."

Gilbert loved a good whiskey. He often took a swig of Father Erlich's private stash disguised in the jumbo mouth wash bottle the priest kept in his medicine cabinet at church.

Maxwell grabbed his arm. "And I can show you my workshop and there's a root cellar next to it to store the vegetables from my garden through the winter. I had to build myself a shed in the back yard because the Little Missus doesn't allot me any work space inside the house."

Gilbert laughed at this apparent reference to Minnie's diminutive stature. Tucking the church key into his pocket, he cast a glance back to the darkened building, then walked off happily with his new best friend.

ᕲ

3

Sunday, March 18

A fter service, Father Lucien stood at the front door shaking hands with parishioners clustered on the church steps and sidewalk to gossip about the whereabouts of Father Erlich. This morning, Saint Bibiana's had been more crowded than usual. The phones had been ringing into the late hours of Saturday night with word Father Lucien would be saying Mass. Those who'd not been seen in church for months woke up early the next morning to be first in the pews.

Invitations to Sunday dinner were graciously extended to the young priest but he'd decided to have his meal alone in the rectory rather than face the thinly veiled interrogation of curious members of his flock. He wouldn't have had much to tell them. Apparently, the office had been robbed and Father Erlich was missing. That was all he knew right now. He'd be speaking with the police later in the afternoon. They'd asked him to come to the station to make an official statement although he had nothing more to add to what he'd given them initially.

He walked across to the rectory and let himself in the front door. A pleasant calmness seemed to have settled over the rooms. He enjoyed having the house to himself. He went into his bedroom, changed into comfortable clothes, and chose some favorite CDs he only listened to in the car. Father Erlich did not like jazz. He also didn't like folk or rock or new age. The old man had two religious choral albums he played when he was in a good mood, but that was the extent of the music allowed in the house.

Lucien turned up the Vince Giraldi disc and went into the kitchen to make lunch. He poured a large glass of juice for himself, which he brought out to the living room where food was not permitted. He sat on the couch and listened to the music while eating his peanut butter and jelly sandwich. Putting his feet up on the coffee table, he couldn't help but think how comfortable he felt. A wave of guilt engulfed him but was promptly extinguished. He murmured, "I could definitely get used to this."

Sunday night, in the auditorium of the Peace Dale Library, what was left of the small band of actors and workers assembled. They were a troupe without a leader and most of the tech crew had abandoned the production. Sophia stood on stage and thanked those remaining for not giving up. "I know the last few weeks have been difficult but we've hired a new director and I'm sure we'll be able to get this show back on track. We've moved the performance dates to the last three weekends in April and I'm confident we'll be set to go by then." She called Ruth to the stage and introduced her.

Ruth said a few words of encouragement and then brought Stewart forward. "This is Stewart Langley, our new Paravicini."

"Ciao miei piccolo amici," Stewart nodded at the dubious younger cast members staring at him and trying to figure out what he'd said.

"Did he just call us pickle friends in Italian?" the character playing Mollie, whose real name actually was Molly, whispered to Reggie, the young man playing her husband Giles.

"Not sure it was Italian but I believe he called us piccolos," Reggie whispered back.

"I think he meant Piccolo. You know, Ma Junior, the black guy in Dragon Ball," Clovis said.

Molly was dubious. "He seems kind of old to be into Japanese animation."

"He's saying hello to you in Italian," Sophia stepped in to explain.

Gino pulled her aside. "See, nobody can unnerstand a word he says. I told ja I shoulda got the part."

Ruth hastily thrust a script in Stewart's hands, opening it to the page where he would first make his entrance.

Sophia looked around at the players on stage. "Where is Major Metcalf?"

"The guy playing him left for a better part in a musical another community theatre group is doing," Clovis said. They all looked to their new director for a solution to the latest problem.

Ruth thought quickly. "Wait a second. I'll be right back."

Her good friend Arthur Jacobs and his two sidekicks, Samuel Hazard and Clay Van Zinck, had come along as enthusiastic volunteers willing to help with any tasks needing to be done. Right now they were searching through the cavernous cellar for props and set pieces from past shows which could be repurposed for this production.

Ruth ran downstairs and pulled Arthur aside. "Could you do me a big favor? I've been informed the person playing Major Metcalf has left for greener pastures. Would you consider taking over the part?"

"Why, I've always wanted to act on stage," he declared looking at his buddies who were nudging each other, showing some doubt as to his ability to handle the challenge. He whispered to Ruth, "I'll learn all my lines tonight. I won't let you down."

"I'm sure you'll be a quick study, Arthur. Thanks for filling in at this late date." Ruth gave him a grateful hug.

They were well into the first scene when one of the flats fell over, narrowly missing Molly and Reggie. "We're okay! No harm done," Reggie assured them as Clovis helped him hoist the wall back into place.

"I swear this play is cursed. You'd think we were doing a production of *Macbeth*," Sophia complained to Ruth.

"Maybe you should avoid saying that here," Ruth warned her. "It's supposed to bring on disaster if you even mention the name of the play out loud in the theatre or quote from it out of context. The Curse of the Scottish play it's called."

"I believe the disaster has already occurred. What else can happen that could be any worse?" she asked not realizing how ominous her words were at the time.

"Sophia, let's not tempt fate," Rick advised as he walked by with a can of paint for the backdrop behind the large windows centered on the rear wall.

"You never struck me as someone who was superstitious, Rick."

"Let's say I like to cover all my bases and play it safe," her brother-in-law said as he did a quick side step to avoid walking under the ladder Gino was setting up.

The gang of four had spent the earlier part of the evening at the Elks Hall. Annette and Howard arrived and she was sporting a large diamond engagement ring. It was unanimously decided to offer a toast to the happy couple.

"Have you set a date?" Doreen asked.

"We'd scheduled an appointment with Father Erlich at Saint Bib's this afternoon but it was canceled," Annette explained. "Father Lucien assured us they'd call when Father Erlich had returned."

"Returned from where?" Darlene was curious.

"Father Lucien didn't say."

"I thought it was strange Erlich wasn't at Mass this morning," Cheryl commented.

Minnie stopped drinking to add, "Maxwell said the police were at the church last night and Lucien told him there'd been a break-in. I wonder if Father Erlich ran off with the church funds?" This new revelation piqued everyone's interest and they began to discuss where the priest could have gone with their money.

"Well, if it means we've gotten rid of him and Father Lucien is in charge, I say it was worth the price of a Sunday's collection," Darlene declared and they all nodded in agreement.

"I never liked that guy," Doreen said. "Two years ago I asked him if he'd baptize my grandson and he told me he hadn't seen my son in church lately. I told him Larry had married his partner Duane and they'd moved out of state. They'd adopted a little boy and were returning to Rhode Island so the baby could be baptized in the church where Larry grew up. Well, you'd think I'd slapped the man in the face. 'Your son is gay?' He yelled at me like I'd committed original sin right there in the church. 'Tell him he's not welcome here!' And he stormed out of his office leaving me sitting alone feeling guilty."

"I never knew. I wondered why you stopped coming to Mass," Cheryl patted her friend's hand.

"Some Sundays I like to try out different churches and I'm in a book group I really enjoy at the Peace Dale Congregational Church."

Annette's fiancé excused himself and went off to use the lav.

"Men, they're all useless," Minnie jumped into the conversation. "If they'd let women be priests, there wouldn't be any of the problems we're seeing right now in the church." She took a long sip from her glass, and declared, "Here's to the Year of the Woman!"

They raised their glasses in a salute. "Amen!" Cheryl said.

"So, where do you think Erlich's disappeared to?" Darlene asked.

"I don't know, but it's no great loss to Saint Bib's. Good riddance, I say," Doreen held up her pint of Guinness stout and they all clicked their glasses in a toast.

"Good riddance!" they hooted in unison.

Eventually, Annette and Howard left and the group piled into Cheryl's car to drive the short distance to Darlene's where they spent the rest of the night around the dining room table bent over adult coloring books, avidly concentrating on staying in the lines. Except for Minnie. She was bearing down on her pencil almost ripping through the page, and with every swig of her gin and tonic, she ventured further and further outside the margins.

"Shhlerry, tossh shat purple penshil over here, wouldja?"

"Minnie, whoever heard of a purple cat? Use this," Doreen said rolling the yellow pencil she'd been using on her daffodils across the table.

"I shee purple cats in my dreamsh all the time. An aqua an lime green an fluschia. I mean fulshia ... ummmm, bright pinky purple."

"How much do you drink before you go to bed?" Darlene glanced up from the page on which she was coloring a hot air balloon.

"I always have a shlot of whishkey with a beer shaser every night at leven thirty on the dot." Minnie accented her statement with a nod, a hiccup, and a resounding belch. "I shleep like a log."

"I enjoy a mug of hot milk before I turn off the lights. It relaxes me," Cheryl said.

"I tried that onesh but it didn't tashte sho good with whishkey." Minnie was starting to slide under the table and Darlene and Doreen each grabbed an elbow to straighten her up in the chair.

"Maybe we should call it a night?" Cheryl suggested.

They agreed and started to collect their things. It was taking Minnie somewhat longer to pack up. Darlene held the tote open while her friend dropped in her coloring book and each pencil one at a time.

"Do you want to sleep on my couch tonight?"

"Nahh! I kin make it home myshelf. I'll cut through the shlemetary."

Darlene pictured her friend tripping around the historic Riverside graveyard and falling into a freshly dug hole. She opened the cellar door. "Gilbert! Turn that radio off. Gilbert, I need you to walk Minnie home," she called down the stairs. When there was no answer, she shut the door. "He must have fallen asleep. Never mind, I need some fresh air," she said as she took a firm hold of her inebriated friend's arm.

"I'll give her a ride," Cheryl offered.

"You're my besht friends." Minnie planted a sloppy kiss on Darlene's cheek. "I jusht love our little parties!"

"Let's see if she feels the same way tomorrow morning," Cheryl whispered to Doreen as they helped get Minnie down the front steps to the car.

❧

4

Monday, March 19

"Ohhhhhhh. Ahhhhhhhh. Noooooooooo! Maxwell, don't raise those the shades."

Her husband moved to the bed and looked down at her. "Minerva, get up. It's almost noon."

His wife pulled the duvet over her head and continued to groan from beneath the covers. "Stop yelling at me. Can't you see I'm in pain?"

He lowered his voice to a whisper. "Then stay in bed the rest of the day for all I care. Your girlfriends have been calling asking where you are. Apparently, you were supposed to pick them up to go shopping this morning."

"Oh no! The alarm didn't go off. Why didn't you wake me up?" She poked her head out and looked at the clock, which confirmed it was indeed almost noon.

"Isn't that what I'm doing right now?" Her husband returned from the adjoining bathroom with a glass of something fizzy and told her to drink it. "And I suggest a hot shower. You smell like a brewery," he said as he left the room.

She moved her head on the pillow and the room swirled around in dizzying circles. Closing her eyes tightly, she rose from the bed and groped her way to the shower. She dropped her flannel nightgown on the floor and stepped in, letting the water wash over her.

"I'm never drinking again," she whined at the cat sitting on the edge of the tub watching her.

"Meow!"

Minnie called Darlene to say she'd be over to pick them up in five minutes. They were in the front yard when she pulled into the driveway twenty minutes later. "Sorry, I couldn't find my keys," she said as they piled into the car.

"Nice shades," Doreen looked at the others knowing Minnie's eyes must have been bloodshot behind her designer sunglasses.

"Where are we going?" Darlene had called shotgun while they waited. She settled into the front passenger seat.

"Shopping for our Easter bonnets. I know a woman in East Greenwich who makes the most darling little hats. Fascinators, they're called. It's all the rage in Britain."

"I like that the Queen always wears a matching hat with her outfits. I think it's real classy. Does she wear fascinators?" Doreen asked.

"No, not her, but the princesses and duchesses do. The younger members of the royal family are not as stodgy as the Queen. Did you know the Royals are required to wear hats at all official occasions. It's a tradition dating back to before the 1950s when upper class women rarely showed their hair in public." Minnie was obviously enjoying the opportunity to display her knowledge of the history of haute couture across the pond.

Doreen wasn't easily impressed. "Sounds like a stupid rule to me. I thought we were going to the bowling alley for lunch. I'm hungry."

"There's a cute little French café next door to the millinery shop. We can eat there after we pick out our chapeaus," Minnie told her.

"I thought we were buying hats. I didn't bring a lot of money with me," Cheryl said.

"I haven't been to East Greenwich in years," Doreen commented. "I always say if you can't get something you need in town, then you don't really need it."

"You and half the population of South Kingstown," Minnie said disgustedly. "There's a whole world outside of Peace Dale and Wakefield. You'd be amazed at what you could experience if you ever left your own backyard. And for your information, *chapeau* means hat in French," Minnie haughtily told her unsophisticated friend.

"I can experience as much of the world as I want on TV, thank you very much. *The Real Housewives of Atlanta. Real Housewives of New Jersey. Real Housewives of Beverly Hills. The Real Housewives of Dallas.*" Cheryl leaned forward in her seat to be closer to Minnie's right ear. "And I don't need to be driving around the state searching for stuff I can find right in my own backyard at Kenyon's Department Store."

"Well, maybe I should just drop you off here and you can walk home while the rest of us buy clothes which won't be exactly the same as the other people in the church pews on Easter Sunday?"

Darlene realized Minnie was obviously still hung over and a bit testy, so when the car began to slow down, she decided to mediate before Cheryl was dumped out by the side of the road. "This is going to be fun! I'm up for a little adventure, myself. And East Greenwich is only twenty minutes away."

Cheryl sat back huffily and looked out the window as the car picked up speed.

Doreen decided to help by changing the topic. "Has anybody heard more about Father Erlich?"

"Nothing. It's as though he's dropped off the face of the earth," Darlene said.

"It's like our own local mystery. Maybe we could go looking for him?" Minnie suggested. "I heard from the church secretary he has a sister in Cumberland, at Mount Saint Rita Health Center."

"The one who's a nun?"

"She's a Sister of Mercy," Doreen offered. "She's his only living relative from what I've been told and is quite ill. The police are checking on if he may have gone to visit."

"What happened to the nurse who took care of him when he was in rehab? I remember she brought him to church a few times. I always thought the woman was sweet on him," Cheryl said.

The comment left them speechless until Minnie glanced back at her in the rear-view mirror. "Well, we're gonna have to get you two hats. One for each of your heads. Who in their right mind would be interested in that wrinkled old coot?"

Maxwell and Gilbert were at the kitchen table eating cheesecake topped with fresh cream and cherries.

"This is fantastic, Maxwell. The best! You should think about setting up a teashop in the village. You could make a small fortune."

"We already have Sweet Cakes. And I like to bake as a hobby. I don't want to have to work at it."

"You've got a lot of hobbies. It makes me feel like I'm wasting my life away. All I do is wander around. I do a little flower gardening. Annuals, mostly. And I spend some of my time at the church. I'm told I'm a good listener. That would be my biggest asset, I guess. But I don't have the creative touch for anything you'd call practical."

"I could show you how to do electrical work and you could help me with the lighting for the play at the library."

"I tried doing stuff around the house once and almost set the place on fire fixing a switch that was on the fritz. It still doesn't work. Darlene's the one who changes the light bulbs when they burn out."

"Minerva likes to dabble with electricity, too. Her father was in the trade, although she'd like people to believe her family is from old money. She taught me all I know. Maybe you could take one of my classes at the Peace Dale Guild?"

"I love the Guild. Mother told me she learned how to cook there. They had classes for the local housewives who were changing from cast iron stoves to the more modern appliances. Some of the women were new immigrants who were learning about American stoves and recipes."

"It's always been a center for learning. Kids used to walk down the street from the high school for their home economics and shop classes. You might be good with carving. It doesn't involve any special tools except for a knife and you can have one of mine. Here," he reached into his pocket, "I've got plenty."

"Thanks." The jackknife snapped open. He looked at the palm of his hand in surprise as blood began to ooze from the cut. "Wow, that's sharp."

Maxwell grabbed a paper towel. "Hold this a minute 'til I get you a plaster."

When he returned, he put antiseptic on the gash and two large band-aids. "I should have warned you. I can't tell you how many times I've cut myself over the years."

"No harm done. It's just a little nick. What kind of stuff do you do?"

"Things you can use around the house." Maxwell pointed out the wooden spoons and the homemade breadbox and spice rack over the stove.

"Looks complicated to me."

"You could start with an easy project." He left the room and came back with some toy trucks, doll furniture, and miniature birdhouses. He opened a box filled with trinkets and unfinished jewelry.

Gilbert touched some loose red and black beads. "They'd make a great rosary," he said. "Darleen collects rosaries."

"Do you like these? They're from a broken bracelet. I found it in Minnie's bureau. If you want, I'll help you string them into prayer beads."

"It's her birthday on Friday. I usually take her out to celebrate the next day. I'd like to surprise her with a gift this year. She's going to be sixty."

"We can start on it today. I've got everything we need in my workshop. I have two classes at the Guild. One is working on decorating Easter eggs we've carved and the other is crafting jewelry. You should stop by on Wednesday. I'll be there most of the day. Ask at the front desk and they'll direct you to where I am." He poured out more whiskey into their shot glasses and then held his up in a toast. "Salut."

"Wow, that's good booze. Better than the stuff Erlich keeps at the church in his Listerine bottle.

"How do you know about that?"

He thought quickly. "Um, I had to use the bathroom once when I dropped something off at the office. The secretary told me I could use it."

Maxwell put another slice of cheesecake on his friend's plate. "Do you want me to show you how to bake?"

"Naw, that's okay. I'd rather just eat. This is the best cake I've ever had. I could never cook like you. But thanks, anyways."

Gilbert took a large forkful of the creamy dessert and let it linger, melting on his tongue for a few seconds before swallowing. "I'm glad you're not the kind of Catholic who gives up sweets and liquor for Lent."

"At this time in my life, the only thing I'd give up for Lent would be my wife," Maxwell chuckled. "And my relationship with whiskey is never on the rocks. It's straight up!"

"That's a good one. I always tell people to drink whiskey for their mental health. It's not good to keep things bottled up." Gilbert was pleased he had something funny of his own to add to the conversation.

Maxwell laughed and slapped him on the back.

Gilbert smiled to himself. He'd said something clever. Maybe Maxwell would visit him in his man cave? He imagined him sitting in the folding chair. This could be the start of a beautiful relationship. His mind wandered and in his thoughts he saw Minnie moving in with Darlene and he and Maxwell staying here together forever. His new best friend poured him a large glass of whiskey. *I could really get used to this.* And Gilbert began to think of ways to get rid of Minnie, smiling to himself as his imagination took flight.

༄

5

Wednesday, March 21

Maxwell's students were adding the finishing touches to the etched wooden Easter eggs they'd been working on for the past week. Gilbert sat observing the class. His new friend was patient and took time with each student to help and encourage them with their projects. Maxwell gave Gilbert one to paint. He was diligently working on it long after the rest of the group had left.

"I like the combination of purple, red, and orange you chose. Very bold," Maxwell said. "We have a special closet for our projects. You can leave yours in there to dry and retrieve it later next week, if you'd like."

"I'll make sure I pick it up before Easter." Gilbert proudly placed the egg carefully on the shelf.

"The Jewelry Crafting Class meets in an hour. There are quite a few students but they've been working on their projects for the last three weeks and don't need much help. You forgot this in my workshop." He handed a box to Gilbert. In it was the rosary. "You need to carve a crucifix. I can spend time with you this afternoon finishing it."

"Thanks, Maxwell. You're a good friend."

People began to collect their tools and pack their projects away.

"Usually I have lunch on the front steps when it's nice out. I made an extra sandwich for you."

The two men sat on the stone steps and Maxwell handed Gilbert a neatly wrapped packet from his lunch box. "It's spam, my favorite. I use spicy hot mustard to perk it up a bit."

Gilbert took a bite. "Ummm. This is real good. I like spam almost as much as I like tuna. Darlene doesn't allow either in the house."

Maxwell passed him the thermos and he took a chug of iced tea. "I put in a little fresh mint from my herb garden." Gilbert high-fived his approval. He looked around at the stone buildings. "They don't make 'em like they used to."

"Yup. They were real craftsmen in those days. When I was a kid, my mom would walk me around the neighborhoods." He looked across to the Village Green where children ran around frolicking on the slides and the swings. "There were no playgrounds. We ran around in the streets. But my mother loved to go for strolls and tell me about her family roots. I'd tag along listening to her tell me all about the history of the village."

"I remember you telling me your mother was a Hazard."

"Her great aunt Mary Peace was the wife of Rowland Hazard. He named the village after her. Four generations of the Hazard Family went into building Peace Dale around the textile manufacturing business they started back in the 1800s."

"My favorite building's the library. The Daniel Chester French bas relief of *The Weaver* in front of the building was commissioned by Caroline Hazard in 1920 to honor the memory of her father and her brothers."

"I know. My mother made me memorize the inscription." Gilbert stood up straight to recite the lines he remembered from his childhood:

"Life Spins the Thread Time Weaves the Pattern God Designed
The Fabric of the Stuff He Leaves to Men of Noble Mind."

"That's beautiful, Gilbert. Your mother would be proud you've remembered those wise words after all these years."

"We would stand in front of those words and when I got it right, she would take me over to the water trough where I'd sail my boat. I loved the fact the trough had three levels, although I could only ever reach into the lower basin where the smaller animals stopped to drink. The top was for horses and the middle for oxen," Gilbert said.

"I overheard a student telling someone his great grandfather was the local stone cutter who crafted the trough at Hazard Rock Farm. That would have been around 1890. He said the top basin came from granite quarried near Mooresfield. It was placed in front of the library but when they widened the road in 1950, they used a team of oxen to move it."

They finished their lunch as people began arriving for the next class session.

"Well, I'll be at the library tonight to finish the plan for the lighting design. It's for a play. You're welcome to come help me, if you want," Maxwell said.

"Are there any strobe lights?"

"Why?"

Gilbert lifted the cuff of his shirt and showed Maxwell a medical alert bracelet on his left wrist. "I'm an epileptic. I have seizures. It's why I don't drive."

"I see. No, I use Fresnel's, scoops, strip lights and spots. Nothing fancy."

"What time?"

"Around seven. You could be my assistant."

"Thanks, I'd like to help."

"And you can watch the show for free if they ever get it all together. They've had a lot of problems so far. But the new director is doing a good job. Ruth Carnavale. Used to be Ruth Eddleman. She's an English professor at URI."

"I've never seen a stage play. What's it about?"

"It's a mystery. This couple runs an inn and there's a snowstorm and a bunch of people are stuck inside with a murderer on the loose."

"Sounds swell. I like a good puzzle to solve."

"You'll love this one, then. I've read the last act. I had to in order to be able to do the lighting design. But I won't tell you who the killer is. It will spoil the suspense. See you tonight."

∾

Rehearsal was set for seven o'clock but the cast arrived early to run lines with each other. Ruth sat in the auditorium going over some details with Clovis, the props manager, and the other techies.

"The first police whistle sounds when the music ends. Then a series of whistles after the underlined cues in your scripts. The inn sign should be placed on the stairs so it can be clearly seen by the audience. Suitcases must be left here to be brought on stage when the characters make their entrances. Magazines and newspapers also need to be placed on the set."

"It will be all organized on the props table according to when it's needed. There are still some items we have to pick up. The ski poles, the cigar case, the revolver. We'll have everything on this list collected by the next rehearsal," Clovis assured them.

Maxwell interrupted them. "I'm working on the lighting design tonight. This is Gilbert Cheevers. He's going to help me."

"Nice to have an extra hand" Ruth said. "When you have the plan completed, I'll check it over. Don't forget the wall brackets and the table lamp in the last scene. Thanks, everyone." The group broke up and went off to work.

Kara arrived later in the evening with a carton of Dunkin Donuts coffee and Ruth came to help her arrange a small table with snacks.

"It looks like the crew is organized. They almost don't need me," Ruth said.

"Clovis is an efficient stage manager. He's done a great job of overseeing the tech end. So, how do you feel the actors are coming along?" Kara asked.

"I think they'll be fine. I'm going to see if we can rehearse totally off script tonight. You could help with feeding them the lines if they trip up."

Ruth called everyone to the stage and after a pep talk, they began the first scene.

Sitting off to the side of the auditorium, Gilbert was mesmerized by what was happening up on the stage. "It's like a whole other world going on while we listen in," he said.

"Well, this can be your new bailiwick."

"Bailiwick?"

"Yes, I heard you liked to eavesdrop."

Gilbert hung his head and his face flushed bright red.

"Don't worry. I like to listen in on conversations, too. If people don't want you to know their business, they should keep it to themselves, I say." Sensing Gilbert's discomfort, Maxwell changed the subject. "Would you like to read the script? Mine's full of notes on sound and lighting cues, but I can get you another copy."

"No, I think I'll just watch them act it out on stage. Don't tell me who did it. I want to figure it out myself. I appreciate a good mystery. Darlene and me never missed *Murder She Wrote* or *Columbo* and I was pretty good at figuring out who did it."

"Well, if I remember *Columbo* correctly, the audience already knew who did it during the first scenes."

"Yup, they did. But I was also good at figuring out the how and why."

"Then maybe you can tell the cops what happened to Father Erlich?" Maxwell suggested.

"If he's anything like most men, he probably needed to get away for awhile. Darlene thinks he's been kidnapped and is being held for ransom."

"Who would pay to get that guy back? Certainly not his parishioners. In case you haven't heard, they can't stand him."

"Funny, I never thought he was as bad as everyone seemed to say. He keeps to himself, but I don't find anything wrong with that."

"You've got a point there," Maxwell agreed. They both turned towards the sound of a crash on the stage. One of the actors had tripped and fallen.

"Mr. Jacques, can you give us some more light up here?" Ruth called over to him. "Sophia, bring the first aid kit. And someone clean up the blood, please."

"This show has been one disaster after another," Maxwell confided in his friend. "I'll be surprised if anyone makes it out of rehearsals alive."

❧

6

Saturday, March 24

"The baby will be grown and in high school before we agree on a color for this nursery," Stewart declared as they sat around looking at the various hues dabbed on the beige walls of what was once a guest room in the Langley home.

"Color is important in the mental and emotional development of a child during its early years. We want to provide as much visual stimulation as possible during the first months. I have the studies to prove that theory right here in my notes." Sophia held up the bulging loose-leaf binder labeled Baby Langley. "If you want to start over, I can bring in more samples," she offered.

Everyone stifled a groan, knowing they'd already spent days narrowing the current choices down to five possibilities. If they had to begin over, the child would be grown, out of the house, and on her own before the adults agreed on a final choice.

"We've all picked our favorite from the myriad of lovely paint samples Sophia has helpfully provided, so let's take a short break and make a final decision after we've had something to eat," Ruth diplomatically suggested.

"Dat's da best idea I've heard all mornin!'" Gino was the first out the room and downstairs into the kitchen. Stewart put on his favorite apron and they helped to bring out the food.

The friends had shared many a meal and Kara sat contentedly looking at each of them in turn thinking of how they were brought together not so long ago.

When she was an undergrad at the University of Rhode Island, Professor Ruth Eddleman had been her favorite English teacher. Kara graduated and spent her early career as a police officer in New York City. She eventually returned to Rhode Island, where they reconnected at a book club for mystery lovers at the Kingston Free Library. Over the next few years, the two women became best friends. Ruth introduced her to Stewart, a member of the university's science department. It was a perfect match. Kara and Stewart had been married for almost eight years and were expecting their first child, much to the joy of their friends.

The previous December, they'd celebrated Ruth's and Rick's wedding. Gino Carnavale, Rick's twin brother, was married to Sophia, the youngest member of the group. She was the one who loved to organize and they were all more than willing to give her free reign.

With a baby due in May, under Sophia's guidance, they were busy decorating and baby-proofing the house for the new arrival.

Stewart was having a difficult time getting one of the kitchen cupboards open. "I hope none of you wants sugar in your tea, because I have no idea how these baby locks work," he sounded a bit frustrated.

"I will explain it to you once again. It really is quite simple. I would think a brilliant astrophysicist like yourself could figure it out. It's not rocket science," Sophia stated.

"Ay, good one Sophia. Rocket science! Stewart being an astrophysicist. Ats funny." Gino smacked his wife on the back in appreciation and then ducked as she tried to flick her thumb to the side of his head.

Kara laughed and she felt the baby kicking, reminding her of the demands a new little person can make on people already set in their ways. After taking a leave of absence from her job as chief detective on the South Kingstown Police Force, she'd recently returned to work part time. Her partner, Carl Sullivan, had been handling cases along with the rest of her team and they all hoped she would eventually be coming back full time. She'd discussed this with Stewart but hadn't made a final decision

"Have you heard any more news about the priest who's gone missing from Saint Bib's?" Ruth asked.

"Carl usually calls to tell me what's going on, but I think he's making an effort not to bother me with the case. I'm glad his confidence is growing enough to investigate this one on his own," Kara said.

"Let's see how long it lasts," Sophia said. Everyone knows you're indispensable."

At that moment the phone rang and Stewart looked at the caller ID. He handed her the receiver. "It's Carl."

Kara hadn't been to the South Kingstown Safety Complex during the past two weeks. She'd been working at the forensics lab at the university, helping Professor Hill on a case. Leo, the young police dispatcher, greeted her enthusiastically with a big hug and called in to Detective Sullivan to tell him she'd arrived. Sullivan, along with Detective Brown and Sergeant Shwinnard came out of her old office to welcome her. She noticed her name was still on the door.

"If I'd known you were coming in today, I'da baked a cake," Shwinnard said. "But I do have some desserts I made last night."

The team sat around for the first fifteen minutes catching up on news and eating the pastel frosted treats Shwinnard, once a professional pastry chef, had brought in that morning.

The door opened and Captain Lewis walked in. "It's good to see you Detective Langley. I know you've been busy at the lab so I hesitated to have Detective Sullivan call, but it looks like we may need help on this case."

"I heard something about Father Erlich's disappearance. Not much has been in the news. It appears to have been hushed up. I thought maybe the Diocese had stepped in. I'm aware he's gone missing but

I don't know any details. If you could tell me what you have, I'll help in any way I can," Kara said.

"You're right. The bishop's been keeping things quiet," Lewis told her. They're trying to stifle rumors this could be tied to the Tucker boy's disappearance. We all remember how Saint Bibiana's went through a terrible time six years ago when it happened, so you can understand why they're playing this down."

"What do you have so far?" she asked.

"On Saturday evening, a week ago, Father Lucien went in search of the parish's elder priest, Father Erlich. He wasn't in the rectory and it was getting late. Lucien walked next door to the church where he found folders strewn around the office." Sullivan handed her photos of the scene. She carefully looked through them as he continued.

"The safe had been emptied. Here's an accounting of what was taken." Lewis handed her a sheet of paper.

"This seems like a lot of money for a church to keep around."

"Usually a deposit of the Sunday offerings is made on Monday morning, but there'd been a big fundraising auction on Thursday evening and those monies were added into the bag to be brought to the bank in one trip."

"Why wasn't it deposited on Friday?" she asked.

"The church treasurer was out of town for the weekend and Father Erlich felt it could wait until the following Monday."

"There was no sign of a struggle at the scene? No blood?" Kara glanced through the pictures once again.

"None, just the paper mess, a broken mug, the open safe and the chair upended. It has all the earmarks of being staged maybe to cover-up something else," Sullivan said.

"Tell me what you know about Erlich. How has he been acting lately? Anything out of the ordinary?"

"The housekeeper, Mrs. Brody, says he's been distracted in the last month or so. And she's noticed he sleeps later in the mornings. He had a heart attack six years ago and she feels he hasn't been well ever since."

Kara thought for a moment and then said, "He had the attack on the day Anthony Tucker disappeared. They were getting the children ready to board the bus home from Bible school. The driver was new and the head teacher was going over the route with her when the secretary called from the office to tell the teacher, a Miss Chowdry, Father Erlich had taken ill. She left the children with the aides to go to the pastor."

"Yes, it was chaos that day which added to the problems encountered when the investigating officers tried to piece together the boy's movements prior to his disappearance." Sullivan referred to his notes.

"Is Laura Chowdry still at the school?"

Detective Brown jumped in. "Uh huh. Father Erlich never really recovered even though he'd had a pacemaker put in. The younger parish priest, Father Lucien, has been assuming some of the duties usually relegated to the senior pastor."

"In the past few days, I've spoken with most of the parishioners," Shwinnard said. "The women were more forthcoming than the men but it wasn't easy getting information from them. I asked if Father Erlich had been acting differently lately and the men were quick to say he'd always been an odd duck. The women hesitated to say anything bad about him, except that he was set in his ways and sometimes difficult to get along with."

"We're beginning to suspect, from what we've been told, there may be a connection to the disappearance of Anthony Tucker. You worked with the investigating team on the case," Lewis stated.

"I did. Not as a detective. I was still an officer and was assigned to the boy's mother, Marjorie. I truly don't know how she stayed sane during those first terrible days." Kara placed her hand protectively over her stomach. "We never found out what happened to the child."

"The file is still open." Sullivan took a folder from the desk and handed it to her. "Could you look over the notes to refresh your memory? It may be important to this case."

"I can do that, although almost every detail is still etched vividly on my brain."

"Would you speak with Marjorie Tucker again? Sometimes it takes a while for the facts to emerge. Maybe she'll remember something we missed at the time," Lewis said.

"I'll call and see when she can meet with me."

The chief thanked her and returned to his office, leaving the team to go over their evidence with Kara.

Kara returned home to find everyone finishing up the work in the nursery. Rick and Gino were collecting the paint cans and brushes and Ruth and Sophia were folding up the drop cloths they'd used to cover the floor. Each wall had been painted a different color and the ceiling was a deep blue with silver stars cascading around the tiniest sliver of a golden moon.

"Do you like it?" Stewart asked, putting his arm around her.

"I love it!" she said.

"It was Gino's idea," Sophia proudly declared.

"We couldn't decide, so we each painted and autographed one of our own." Ruth pointed to the pale moss green wall signed Auntie Ruth. The signature on the sunny yellow wall was Uncle Rick, on the rosy pink wall, Auntie Sophia, and on the pale violet wall, Uncle Gino.

Stewart nodded to the ceiling and the writing on the tail of the silver meteor.

"Mom & Dad - that would be us," Kara kissed him. "What a lovely room for our little girl."

"On that topic, I've been researching names I think you should consider," Sophia announced. "I'll go and get my notebook."

Gino called after her, "Don't bother, Honey. I'm pretty sure they'll be calling the baby Gina.

On his drive back to the rectory, Father Lucien reflected on the Saturday night dinner party hosted by one of his parishioners. The other guests were curious for information on Father Erlich's whereabouts and were looking forward to hearing Lucien preach the next day. He excused himself early, explaining the need to prepare his sermon. He'd been aware of Erlich's unpopularity but was surprised no one appeared worried about their curate's disappearance. Most assumed he'd absconded with the money.

The phone was ringing as he came through the door but when he picked up the receiver, he was met with silence. "St. Bibiana's Rectory. Father Lucien speaking ... hello? Is anyone there?" A click and then a dial tone. He hung up the phone and checked the caller ID. Unknown.

Lucien stood outside the old priest's bedroom. The police had gone through the closet, the bureau, and desk but found nothing to give them a clue as to where he might be. All of his clothes were pressed, hung and folded exactly as Mrs. Brody had left them on Friday - laundry day. She assured them nothing was missing except the clothes he was wearing on Saturday.

"He didn't own that many outfits," she explained, "and sometimes he wore the same one for days. It was his uniform - black chinos and a white shirt – short sleeved in the summer, long sleeved the other seasons." She pointed out his black oxfords, white cotton socks, and opened his neatly arranged underwear drawer. A black raincoat still hung in the hall closet along with a brown woolen overcoat and on the floor, the grey rubbers he slipped on to protect his shoes in the rain and the snow. He owned two black ties which were tucked into the corner of the top drawer of his bureau along with some silver cuff links and a tie clip he'd been given as gifts but had never worn. A dozen frayed white cotton handkerchiefs mixed in with his collars filled the remaining two drawers.

He stepped into the room and went to the desk. It had only one center drawer and inside were a few Bik pens, six well-sharpened number two pencils, and a church directory which included photos of the members of Saint Bibiana's. Lucien turned on the lamp and touched the blotter which covered the surface of the desk. No doodles or words or numbers marked its green surface. He removed the directory from the drawer. A small stick-it note was taped on the inside back cover with a telephone number and the name Effie. He thought it might be the name of Erlich's sister, a nun who was in a convent nursing home at the northern end of the state. Erlich visited her every Wednesday but never talked about her with the younger priest.

He suddenly realized how much he didn't know about the man. He'd been interviewed and given his official statement but could provide them little information on this person with whom he lived. There was nothing else they shared except the roof over their heads and a vocation to which they'd each dedicated their lives. But the old boy had a very different view of what that vocation entailed.

Erlich never wanted to get close to his parishioners. He did his job and kept a safe distance between him and his flock. On the other hand, the younger priest believed understanding the people he served was the first step in helping them toward salvation. The two priests had little in common except for the parishioners they were sent to serve. The manner in which they each chose to do their jobs was different, but it had seemed to be working well up until now.

Lucien re-opened the directory to the smiling faces in the booklet. Turning the pages, he wondered who among them might have reason enough to want to get rid of their pastor. As he thought more about it, the list of potential suspects grew.

PALM SUNDAY, MARCH 25

A little girl dressed as a donkey led the children into the sanctuary. They proudly marched up and down the aisles waving
their palms. The adults sang and clapped in time along with Father
Lucien's rousing rendition of "When the Saints Come Marching In"
on the trumpet. The pews in the tiny church were filled with parishioners eager to hear what their young priest had to say. Carefully
chosen words which would help ease their minds and soothe their
souls. The children marched out following their teachers downstairs
to Sunday school.

"He reminds me of the Angel Gabriel. Aren't you glad you
decided to come back?" Cheryl whispered to Doreen as they settled
in. Her friend nodded and looked up expectantly at the man in the
pulpit about to begin the Mass.

It hadn't taken long for Lucien to make changes more in keeping
with his own style of pastoring. When it came time for the Prayers
of the People, quite a few members were praying they'd seen the last
of Father Erlich, although no one voiced it out loud.

Midway through the sermon the microphone shut off, but his
voice carried his message to the back of the church where Darlene
was sitting. She put her hand up to shield her lips and leaned over to
Gilbert. "Father Erlich would never have been able to project back
this far." He agreed and checked the bulletin to see how much more
was left in the service.

The offertory baskets were filled to the brim and after the final blessing, smiling parishioners lined up on the church steps to thank Lucien for his words of inspiration. An aura of peace had settled over the church and people left that morning feeling good about themselves and with a sense of hope things were going to get better from now on.

Lucien stored his trumpet back into its case and placed it under his bed. He turned on a jazz album and then changed into comfortable clothes. He walked around in his stockinged feet straightening up the living room before the housekeeper arrived. The bishop had invited himself to dinner and Mrs. Brody happily offered to bake a honeyed ham with hot rolls, whipped potatoes, peas, candied carrots, and a strawberry shortcake for the occasion. She was taking advantage of the fact that even though it was Lent, Sunday was exempt from the old rules of abstaining from meat and dessert. She wanted His Holiness to know, when called upon, she could put a good meal on the rectory table. Lucien extended an invitation for her to join them.

"Ah, no, you two will be needin time to discuss matters which have no concern for the likes of me. I'll just leave ye to it. But I'll be back later on tonight. Don't you worry yerself about the cleanin up. Mind ye, I'll be takin care of that."

He realized she was right and tried to prepare himself for some of the questions his superior would, no doubt, be asking. He wasn't sure what to say, but he'd decided to stick with the facts he'd been given by the police. Father Erlich had disappeared from his office a week ago and money was missing from the safe. (The bishop would want an exact accounting of how much had been taken.) No one had heard from the pastor during the past week and the police were still investigating. His car was parked in the garage and so either he was taken against his will or had left with someone.

There was a knock on the door. It was the church treasurer stopping by to tell the priest he'd counted the collection and it was four times more than their usual Sunday receipts. Lucien thanked him, knowing the bishop would be extremely pleased with that piece of information.

Mrs. Brody arrived just as the phone rang and he'd picked up the receiver on the outdated, push-button telephone. "Saint Bibiana's rectory. Father Lucien speaking."

This was met with silence at the other end.

"Hello? Can I help you?"

More silence. He hesitated, then whispered, "Father Erlich? Are you there?" He stood for a few moments waiting expectantly until the caller suddenly disconnected.

"We'd love to help. What time do you want us there? Okay. See you then." Stewart hung up the phone and went in search of his wife to tell her the good news. She was reading the Sunday paper in the den.

"Carl called. He was planning on taking Jess out for dinner for their anniversary, but the babysitter backed out and his mother has a cold. I told him we'd be glad to take care of the boys. He was relieved and confided in me that from Billy's astute observations, we're the only ones who seem to be able to manage little Connor."

Kara laughed. "It sounds like a good idea to me. What time do they want us there?"

"Around two. Oh, and I suggested he take her out to a movie and maybe go for dessert at Gregg's afterwards."

"Oh, my. That was generous of you."

"I figured we could use all the child-rearing practice we can get before the baby arrives."

"In theory, it appears to be a good plan. But the reality of a whole afternoon and evening with Connor feels somewhat daunting right now."

Stewart and Kara arrived early.

"I really appreciate this," Carl whispered to Kara.

"You behave for Mr. and Ms. Langley. We'll bring you each a special surprise when we come home." Jess hugged the boys and pet the dog's head.

Connor ran to the front window to watch the car pull out of the driveway. When it had disappeared from view, he raced to his parent's bedroom and returned clutching a DVD. *Diehard With a Vengeance.* "My movie. Mommy said so." He handed Kara the box and she examined it carefully.

"Oh my! I don't think there are any animals in this movie. I know how much you love baby sheep and goats." Kara gave her husband a nod and took out a picture book from her bag. "Would you like me to read this to you?"

He looked at the animals on the cover. "Alpacas!" He climbed on to her lap and Billy moved in close to her as his little brother pointed to the pictures in the book of some of the animals he recognized from his visits to Peckham Farm at URI. The dog dropped a chew toy at Stewart's feet and he tossed it across the room watching the clumsy pup tumble after it. He caught his wife's eye and she smiled up at him, both of them thinking of the many Sundays to come with their own child.

༄

Monday, March 26

Carl Sullivan was running late. He'd been helping his wife straighten up the house. The previous night after the Langleys had gone home, the family had put up an Easter tree of silver birch limbs. They'd hung fuzzy yellow chicks next to colorful plastic eggs and had strung twinkle lights among the boughs.

On Monday morning they were awakened by Connor who was standing in the bedroom doorway yelling, "Bad doggie! Bad doggie!" In the living room, they found decorations strewn all over the floor and under the furniture. The little boy began chasing Max around as the puppy retrieved broken branches to bring to the pile he'd started under the kitchen table, the animal's favorite hoarding place.

"We should trade that dog in for a goat," their elder son declared at breakfast as he spread blueberry jam on his English muffin. "It could sleep in the garage, keep the grass trimmed, and we'd be able to recycle all our garbage and tin cans and never have to buy it any food."

Since mowing the lawn had been added to his list of spring and summer chores, Billy had an ulterior motive for wanting to get rid of the present family pet and replace it with a more useful animal.

"I think he's making a good point," Carl whispered to his wife.

"And I think you need a stronger cup of coffee," she whispered and then spoke a little louder. "You know, Carl, I'm not so sure it was the dog that made the mess."

"Maybe we should take these decorations and hang them on the cherry tree in the front yard, so whoever it was who did this can't tear it down again," her husband responded loudly.

"Noooooooooo! No outside! Inside Easter tree!" Connor screamed as he chased Max into the bathroom, closing the door behind them.

Jess and Carl sat down at the table and spent a few minutes savoring their morning coffee.

"Should I go check on him? It's gotten pretty quiet," Carl said.

"Wait another minute or two," Jess told him, refilling her mug.

"I'll bet he's flushing his underpants down the toilet again," Billy warned the adults in the room.

The sound of the toilet flushing motivated Carl to get up from the table to see if water was seeping from under the bathroom door.

Billy looked at his mother and smiled. "We could probably get a whole herd of goats if we throw Connor into the deal."

"I'll keep that in mind," she answered.

Marjorie emptied the rest of her morning coffee into the sink. She looked out to the driveway, watching Louis get into his car to leave for work. He'd aged so much during the past six years. His hair was now almost totally grey. He was becoming more and more forgetful and there were days when he moved stiffly, like an arthritic old man.

She turned to the table to remove the breakfast dishes. One plate was still untouched at the place she always set for Anthony. Every morning, she pretended he was upstairs in his room getting dressed for the day. Like it used to be. They'd argued about it, but Louis soon gave up and let her do as she pleased.

It had been difficult for her husband during those first months. The police always tended to turn to the parents as potential suspects when a child goes missing. But Louis had been at a job, two hours away and numerous witnesses attested to this. Marjorie had been home all day. Her neighbor had been working on tending the trumpet vines and annuals along the front fence, as she did most afternoons, and was certain the boy had never gone past her garden and into his house. The police quickly concluded that Marjorie and Louis had nothing to do with Anthony's disappearance. They pursued other leads, none of which led them to finding the child.

Before she could clear the table, the front doorbell rang and she went to answer it. She remembered the days she'd spent with Officer Langley, the attractive black woman now standing on her stoop. This woman had sat with her for hours, waiting for some word of the boy. Both praying. Neither speaking.

"Hello, Marjorie. I'm a little early. I hope you don't mind," Kara said.

"Not at all. I'm glad to see you. And congratulations. When are you due?"

"In May. Before the heat of the summer, thank goodness."

Kara walked into the kitchen where they'd spent so many days together. She noticed the place setting.

"Let's go out to the patio. The weather has been lovely and I've put in a flower garden back there."

The conversation was filled with talk of the mild March they were now having after the first snow early in the month; how early Easter was this year. And of the daffodils, crocus, and hyacinth which were pushing up through the soil with a promise of yellow and purple blooms soon to follow. The lilac bush by the back door was getting ready to flower.

"I planted bulbs and perennials because I know they'll come back again at this time each spring."

"What are those little blue flowers?"

"*Myosotis sylvatica* - Forget-me-nots."

The tiny blossoms grew wild around a small plaque in the ground with "LuLu" on it. Atop the grave were tiny carved animals; a lion, a giraffe, a black bear, a monkey. Even a garter snake – all standing guard to protect Anthony's beloved pet gerbil. The sense of loss for this family overwhelmed Kara in that instant and she had to look away.

"The yard feels like a park. Your bushes will be blooming early this year."

"When LuLu died, right after Anthony disappeared, the neighbors came over to help plant a garden to welcome him when he came back home. The two of us always went to the azalea gardens to walk around the paths and he'd take photos of every color blossom. His favorites were the orange rhododendrons. He collected the petals which had fallen on the ground and carried them home in the orange baseball cap his dad had bought for him when they took the train to Baltimore to see an Orioles/Red Sox game." She pointed to two budding bushes nearby. "I still visit there each June, to walk among the shrubs." She hesitated. "It's nice to talk about him with someone."

"Marjorie, how are you and Louis doing?"

"We go from day to day. I still hold out hope, but I know Louis has given up. I'm resentful of that. I have to believe I'll see my son again some day."

The two women sat in familiar silence.

"I'm sorry I stopped answering your messages, Kara. I did appreciate knowing you were still thinking of us."

"I was glad you answered the phone this morning. I wanted to find out how you were doing and needed to ask you something," Kara said.

"I suspect it has something to do with Father Erlich. We don't attend church any more. My neighbor told me he's gone missing. Is it true?"

"The police are looking into all aspects of the case."

"Do the police think he was taken against his will?"

"Captain Lewis is leaving the possibility open."

"And that might lead them to believe it could be connected to Anthony's disappearance." She looked questioningly at Kara. "What do you think?"

"Detective Sullivan is in charge of the case. I'm working part time at the department but was asked to assist. If there is a connection, they're hoping I might be able to root out what it is. I was thinking you and I could put our heads together and see if we missed something back then."

"What can I do to help?"

"Go over it with me - everything you can remember from the time Anthony left that morning."

She thought for a while. "Anthony had breakfast and I packed a lunch and put it in his backpack. He ran out of the house but came back in for his cap. I gave him an extra hug and stood on the sidewalk watching as he skipped to the end of the street to meet up with his friend Jody. I waited until they got on the bus together. It was later than on most other days. There was a young, substitute driver, Miss Robinson, and she wasn't familiar with the route. She turned up the street and came right past the house. Anthony waved at me as it went by."

"I remember you telling me the bus usually didn't go up this street."

"No, it was supposed to travel from the school, up through the Oaks, cross back around the Peace Dale Rotary to High Street then to Main and finally turn on to River Street where it went right back toward the church to complete the circuit."

"From the statement of the driver, it's the route she took in the afternoon. A parent had called to complain her son hadn't been picked up that morning and she would be dropping him off. Miss Chowdry intended to speak with Miss Robinson about the matter before they put the children on the bus to go home," Kara said.

"From what we later learned, Miss Chowdry was called back into the church. Father Erlich had been taken ill. The driver said she'd let all the children off the bus before returning to Saint Bib's. She counted them and it was the same as in the morning. She was positive Anthony had gotten off with the other kids. She distinctly remembered his red hair and the Oriole's baseball cap."

"Robinson followed the correct route in the afternoon?"

"Yes, she said Anthony was one of the last to get off the bus. No one saw him after that. By the time Miss Robinson arrived back at the church, the EMT's had stabilized Father Erlich and the ambulance was transporting him to the hospital."

They sat in the garden, with their memories, silently trying to recall if they'd missed anything about that July day.

In the peace and quiet of his office, Carl scanned the stacks of paper covering the surface of his desk. The last time the priest was seen was when he left the rectory on Saturday, March 17. Mrs. Brody, the housekeeper, told them Father Erlich had a light lunch and then left the rectory at 2:00 PM. Brody finished her chores and went home early, around 3:00 PM right after Father Lucien went out on his rounds. The door to the church had been unlocked when Lucien went to find Erlich at approximately 6:30 PM. Sullivan reread Father Lucien's statement stating he arrived in church and found papers on the office floor and the safe open. He phoned the police.

Laura Chowdry mentioned she'd heard a noise overhead while cleaning up the classroom. Clovis Machado had been with Chowdry and was busy folding up the tables and putting them in the storeroom at the time. He said he'd not heard anything unusual before he'd left for the day. Both confirmed the parking lot was empty and no lights were on in the church when they went to their cars - Machado at 3:20 PM and Chowdry at 3:45 PM. Chowdry had waved to someone she thought was peering out behind the rectory curtain.

Sullivan spread the photos taken that day on his desk and examined each one in turn. It still struck him how the room looked like a robbery had been staged. The chair was the heavy, upholstered swivel type and would have been hard to topple.

The next document in the file was a copy of the priest's sermon for Sunday entitled, "Suffer the Little Children". Sullivan read it through twice before something occurred to him. He turned the sheet over. It appeared the sermon hadn't been completed and the word Confess was written in tiny letters on the back of the last sheet. He called Lucien's cell phone.

"Father, this is Detective Sullivan. I wonder if you could tell me when confessions are heard at St. Bibiana's?"

"Fridays at seven o'clock in the Sanctuary. It was one of the duties Father Erlich insisted on doing although I do hear confessions on my visits to the sick and homebound, " the priest explained.

"Do you know which parishioners were in the church on Friday?" Sullivan asked.

"No, I usually make hospital and nursing home visits on Friday and Saturday in the late afternoon and evening. On Friday night, Father Erlich performed the sacrament of Penance - Reconciliation - in church," Lucien said. "When I got back to the rectory, Father was in his study writing his sermon. I checked on him before I went up to my room to read."

"Did he say anything to you about his day? About confessions?"

"He wouldn't share that with me or anyone else. We're bound by the seal of the confessional under pain of excommunication. He didn't have much to say, as usual. He told me he'd be working for at least another hour and to lock up for him."

"Thank you. If you think of anything Father Erlich may have mentioned, please call me and I'll be in touch if we get any more news."

When he hung up, he sat re-reading the sermon, turning it over to look at the one word on the back of the final sheet. It seemed to him the words had been written with someone specific in mind. Someone who probably sat in the church every Sunday. But this was a sermon which wouldn't be delivered. It very well could be the last sermon the good father would ever write.

Yak, yak, yak yak, yak! "You didn't put the garbage out in time to be picked up. I should make you haul it to the landfill yourself! Why are there dirty dishes in the sink? Do I look like your maid? You tracked mud all over my clean floor. I'm expecting my friends and the place is a mess. You belong in a barn!" Darlene was revved up and her motor was racing.

He was trying to let it go in one ear and out the other but it got stuck in his head. A veritable traffic jam of complaints stalled inside his brain. Like that song, "Don't Worry, Be Happy". He'd hear it on the radio and it stayed with him all week. At times like this he actually preferred the dumb song to her grating voice. Gilbert hummed a few bars, but his wife's nagging just kept drowning it out. You had to hand it to the woman, she was good at this! Besides, he was still angry with her. She'd blabbed to her friends about his listening to confessions. Pretty soon the whole church would know.

"I think it's time for another vacation," he muttered to himself as he grabbed his backpack from the hall closet and headed out the door. He could still hear Darlene going on as he went down the steps. Blah, blah, blah, blah, blah. She probably wouldn't even realize he wasn't in the house for days.

From across the street, Gilbert looked cautiously around the parking lot. It was empty and he sensed it was safe to let himself into the basement with his key. Saint Bib's had been swarming with police for the past week. Darlene's yappy friends were all busy on the phone lines and from what he'd heard, Father Erlich had taken off with the loot. His own parents had made sure he'd had a strong, parochial education under the watchful eyes of the nuns. He grew up in the enveloping arms of the Catholic Church so nothing these priests did could surprise him.

He'd bumped into the good Father twice when he was "vacationing" in the church and on those occasions the priest had never bothered to give him the time of day. He'd had a close call on the Saturday the priest disappeared. Erlich had come into his office and didn't realize Gilbert was in the adjoining bathroom. Erlich didn't appear to notice anything amiss and, as the interloper hid behind the bathroom door, the priest had made a phone call.

Gilbert had learned something new from the conversation he'd inadvertently overheard. He'd thought priests couldn't share anything they'd heard in the confessional, but apparently, this was not the case. Erlich was talking about something that, from his tone, had been bothering him. Gilbert wondered, at the time, how many people confessed their adulterous acts to a priest when they had no intention of ending the affair. Erlich hung up suddenly and left to go into the Sanctuary. Gilbert remembered beating a hasty retreat to his regular hiding place in the back of the storeroom, stopping at the refrigerator to grab a piece of fruit.

Gilbert stopped into the priest's office to get a quick nip of whiskey from the medicine chest. It was nice to have a bathroom to himself that didn't smell of hairspray. He went into the outer office and through the hall into the kitchen. It was Monday night. The secretary had left for the day, so the coast was clear. He was hoping for another tuna fish sandwich left over from the previous Friday but the contents of the refrigerator proved a bitter disappointment.

He removed two slices from the loaf of bread and in the top closet he found the jars of peanut butter and grape jelly to make himself a pbj sandwich. He licked the knife clean before putting it back into the drawer, and then went out to the Sanctuary to make himself comfortable in his pew and wait for the choir members coming in for their practice that evening.

He lay back, propping his head up on his backpack, settling in and opening up the hymnal, flipping through the pages, humming some of the old familiar songs. "Nearer my God to Thee, La, La, La, La, La, La La, La, La ..." The church was quiet and peaceful. He wasn't worried at all and he felt pretty damn happy. Life was good.

Ruth could hear a familiar voice coming from the church's sanctuary. Her good friend, Joan Henderson was speaking with a young couple.

"Peace Dale Congregational was an historic church which began as a Sunday School organized by Margaret Rood Hazard and her husband Rowland Hazard II in their home. The European architectural style building itself was completed in 1872. Their daughter, Caroline Hazard, a past president of Wellesley College, continued the philanthropy her family had begun long after her parents were gone. That stained glass rose window was designed by John La Farge the painter who came to Rhode Island to study with William Morris Hunt in Newport."

The young woman chimed in, "I recognize the name from my Art History class. John La Farge lived in Newport. Wasn't he involved in a controversy with Louis Tiffany?"

"Yes, but they were friends, before all the trouble started. It was La Farge who first introduced the use of opalescent glass and began to create windows with the material. It completely changed the thousand-year-old art of stained glass."

"Why did they end up enemies?"

"La Farge claimed a young Tiffany visited him around 1870 and he'd shared his experiments with layering sheets of the opal glass. Tiffany was totally taken with the color effects and went on to add layers of air space between the panels. He patented this technique. But La Farge had also patented the first use of the glass to be manufactured for windows. They both claimed precedence and exclusivity for the creating of their glass windows."

"Was the dispute ever settled?" the woman asked.

"Not really. The difference in the patents was one of construction – La Farge's for the use of the material and Tiffany's for its assembly. Both men were dependent on each other in order to legally make their designs. A partnership was suggested and La Farge supposedly waived his rights to the formula. But the eventual failure to launch a business together caused friction between the two until La Farge's death."

Joan noticed Ruth and waved. Joan escorted the couple to the front of the church and they thanked her as they left.

Ruth glanced around at the stained glass windows. "I'm always fascinated by the amount of history you have stored away ready to share. The rose window is particularly lovely."

"I love to watch how it changes with the light during the passing hours of the day," she told Ruth. "We look upon such beauty and few people ever know the contentious history behind it all. To most, it's a marvelous piece of art which fills us with a sense of awe when the sun streams through to bring color into our lives."

"And has your life been colorful since our last meeting?" Ruth asked with a chuckle.

The two women walked to the meeting room chatting about what they'd been doing during the past month. The group soon began arriving. It had grown since Joan had taken over. She had a knack for attracting people to her and explained this special talent once to Ruth. "Dearie, when you're an only child, you have to be able to make friends or you'll spend most of your childhood alone."

"I've enjoyed the theme you've chosen for our books this year. I made a list of some other works dealing with looking back at the past that the group might want to tackle in the future." Ruth handed her a folded sheet of paper.

"Thanks. I recognize most of these tiles. I'll make copies of this for the others and we can decide which ones we'd like to read."

One of Joan's favorite things was leading the book group's discussion. Tonight, she decided they would be centering on a quote within a chapter entitled "The Republic of Gilead" in Margaret Atwood's *A Handmaid's Tale*. She'd chosen it because she empathized with the women characters who'd been placed in a subservient role by the patriarchy existing within the book's pages. She'd been a young wife back in the 1950s and her first husband had been adamantly against her returning to college to get a degree in nursing. The theme of the novel, the repression of women, was something she'd could readily identify with and she knew she could offer some personal input on how religious perspectives in the role of women had evolved or had not.

Joan read aloud from the chapter in which the main character, Offred, is thinking back on a conversation with her husband Luke. "We thought we had such problems ... How were we to know we were happy?" She bookmarked the page. "Have you ever thought back on the past and realized you were not aware, at the time, of how good you had it?"

The group shared situations when this had happened in their lives. Many of the examples centered around love ones who had died and were missed. Joan could empathize with all of them as she sorely missed her second husband Norman. They'd had a good life together and she would have liked more years spent with this kind man who'd shown her that not all husbands were as tyrannical as her first had been. She'd eventually returned to college to get her master's degree and now, could scarcely identify with the young, naïve bride she'd been back in the fifties. After they'd exhausted their thoughts on this topic, Joan decided to change course.

"Perhaps we might discuss times which, in hindsight, were not so good?" she suggested.

"I have a situation when I think back to my previous church," one of the women said. "I didn't know how bad it was until I got out and visited other churches." Most of the group knew she'd come from Saint Bib's and were curious about what she meant.

"What makes you think it was so much worse, Doreen?" Joan asked.

"The priest there is the most self-centered person I've ever met. He makes me wonder how someone could serve a congregation and be totally obsessed with his own wants and needs. But that's how he's been lately. The constant whining about being unappreciated is the center of each one of his sermons," she explained. "He seemed to blame all of us for making him exhausted and sick."

Her husband jumped in, "The man's taken to carrying around antiseptic pads to clean his hands if anyone so much as brushes by him. A regular Lady Macbeth. Every week there'd be less and less people showing up on Sunday mornings."

Joan had developed a deep understanding of self-absorbed men but age had mellowed her feelings. "Sometimes too much can be expected of church leaders. Did anyone speak to him about this? Maybe something was bothering him? And I'm sure he would have appreciated thoughtful feedback on his sermons. We all need constructive criticism at times."

"Father Erlich didn't welcome criticism, constructive or otherwise and he wasn't open to anyone's advice, especially if it came from a female," Doreen declared.

"She's right. I'm surprised there's a woman left in the church," her husband added.

Another joined in. "I found his treatment of women bordered on abusive. Two of the ladies who were on the church council left because of his behavior. Whenever they would bring him a concern from the congregation, he became defensive. 'I'm the priest and if anyone has something to say, they should call me on my cell, not discuss it with you people,' he'd told them." She'd become quite animated in relating the situation and when her friend put a hand on her shoulder, she primly settled back down to compose herself.

"Well, I think this might be an appropriate time to say a special prayer for the good father. He probably could use some positive thoughts to guide him on his journey through life's difficult valleys." Joan bowed her head and they joined hands.

On the way out of the meeting, Ruth overheard a comment from Doreen's husband.

"Maybe if we say another prayer, Erlich will come back from his life journey through the Connecticut Wine Valley before he's gambled away all of Saint Bib's money at the casinos?"

"If that's where he is, I'd rather he keep the money and never come back," she told him.

Ruth tucked away the information to share with Kara the next day.

9

TUESDAY, MARCH 27

K ara once again looked through the photos of the church office. "I think you're right. This robbery appears to be staged. Some valuable items were left inside the safe. Only the money was taken."

"Even if the thieves didn't want to try and pawn them, they could have been melted down for the silver," Sullivan said.

"I agree with you but what about the priest? Was it staged to cover up his kidnapping? His car is still parked at the rectory. And if he was the one who planned the whole thing, then he either walked away or someone picked him up," Kara said.

"If he was kidnapped, do you think he's still alive?" Sullivan asked. "It's been ten days and no ransom note, no call, no sign of him."

"It's not that easy to stash a body for long in a village," Shwinnard said.

"I keep going back to the sermon. It felt like it had been written with someone specific in mind. He turned the sheet over to show them the word which had caught his attention. I got to thinking about the things priests are privy to and I ran a check on who was in the church for confessions - a few women and one guy - a Gilbert Cheevers. One of the women tells me he's there every Friday right next to the confessional booth. She said she'd recently heard that he listens in on people's sins. It didn't seem to bother her. She said she really doesn't have much to confess at her age but she and her friends usually stop by the church after they bowl on Friday evenings. They're regulars."

"Was Cheevers helpful?" Kara asked.

"I haven't been able to track him down. I stopped by the house twice, but his wife said he wasn't home. She told me he spends a lot of time walking around the village. She took me to his man cave in the cellar. It wasn't much to write home about. A chair, a fridge, an old TV set. I'll check in again this week and see if he's around," Sullivan said.

"You know, there's always the possibility Erlich may have absconded with the money, himself. Ruth overheard a comment at her book club. Something about the priest gambling. Has anyone you've interviewed mentioned anything along those lines?"

"Father Lucien said Erlich had taken some trips to the casinos a few years back, but not recently. He didn't have many fans in the congregation, although most people did agree it was only in the past few years he'd soured. From what I can surmise, he wasn't as bad during the first three years he was assigned to the parish. After his heart attack, he became pretty cantankerous, if we can believe the parishioners we interviewed," Shwinnard said.

"Did you check with his relatives?"

"Mrs. Walters, the secretary, told us he has a sister who's a nun. We called the convent and they informed us he hadn't been to visit for a while."

"Maybe we should extend the search into Connecticut, to the casinos, to see if he's sitting at some slot machine or black jack table? Do you want to take a ride with us?" Sullivan offered.

"I think I'll pass. Gino talked us into going to a concert at Foxwoods last year. The show was great but walking through the casino was extremely depressing. Old people sitting there like zombies feeding the quarter slots. Some of them hooked up to portable oxygen tanks. And I thought the constant pinging sounds coming from those machines would drive me insane. I don't want to take the chance and subject my unborn child to that," she chuckled. "Besides, I'm meeting Marjorie Tucker today. You're on your own."

"Then, I guess it's just you and me," Carl said to his sergeant. "Grab your nickels, Shwinny! Baby needs a new pair of shoes!"

∽

Marjorie was already waiting for her at the Kinney Azalea Gardens. Kara took the picnic basket from her back seat and walked the short distance to where they'd chosen to meet. She was sitting on a bench with her eyes closed as if in meditation and Kara quietly sat down next to her. Buds were already formed on the bushes. It wouldn't be long before the garden was filled with daily visitors walking along and lounging on the grass among the rhododendrons, azaleas, camellias, their blooms opening up over the course of the springtime. The pale pinks, fuchsias, purples, ivories, reds, yellows, white, and orange limbs would form an honor guard along the paths to welcome visitors into their sanctuary.

"This is so peaceful," Kara said.

"Anthony loved the Pixie Path and the Troll Bridge," Marjorie answered without opening her eyes. "I still picture him stooping to examine a jack-in-the pulpit or a lily-of-the-valley and explaining that the pixies who lived under the bridge used the tiny petals as caps. He had such a vivid imagination. I think he would have become writer - or a botanist. He adored flowers and plants." Kara put her arm around the still grieving mother and they sat in companionable silence as they had years before.

Kara closed her eyes too, remembering when her mother had brought her and her sister, Celia, to the Spring Tea always held by the Kinneys each May on the Saturday before URI's graduation. Lorenzo Kinney's wife loved the azaleas in her native Virginia and her nostalgia for the colorful southern bushes caused her husband to plant some on their property, eventually hybridizing them to survive in the versatile New England climate. Kara had stopped going to the gardens when her mother fell into a deep depression after Celia died.

Marjorie reached into the pocket of her sweater and brought out frayed photos of Anthony peeking around the stone moon gate. She cradled them in her hands, passing them one at a time to her friend.

Kara knew these pictures had been worn by constant handling much like the one she kept in her wallet. It had been taken on a bright, sunny morning – she wasn't sure of the day. Her mother had dressed them up with hats and gloves and patent leather shoes. She brought them to the garden to take a snapshot of her sister and her standing in front of the Oriental Outpost Shed next to the bright pink blossoms her sister loved so much. Afterwards, they'd gone for a surprise lunch, her mother cautioning them not to spill on their Sunday best. It had been one of the memories she kept tucked away when she thought of her childhood and how soon it had ended with her sister's death.

Kara looked at the little boy's image proudly standing in front of his favorite orange azalea bush. "Tell me about him again."

"Anthony loved flowers and bedtime stories and music. He had a little music box with a key. He would wind it up and dance around his room to the melody. If I heard it, I would go upstairs and he would bow and ask if he could have the pleasure of the next waltz. He was a strange little kid – old beyond his years."

"Did you keep his things?"

"Yes, his room is the same as the morning he left. I can't bear to think of changing it. I leave his door slightly ajar, waiting to hear the music box play again some day. Then I'll know this was all a terrible nightmare and everything will return to the way it was. I pray every night for a second chance." She rested her head on Kara's shoulder. "I always kept him close to me. Never let go of his hand in a store, on a sidewalk, in a parking lot. I thought I was keeping him safe but I lost him." For the longest while, Kara let her cry, knowing this woman grieved silently every day even though years had passed and life had continued on.

"No one should have to suffer like this. I need to know where he is. I feel he's close by. Please help me find him … even if …." Marjorie gave her one of the photos.

Holding the memory of this little boy in her hand, Kara promised her friend she would do everything she could to discover what had happened to her son.

Father Lucien was in the church office getting the bulletin ready for Easter Sunday. He called out to the secretary, "Would you check to see if Weedweavers billed us for the Easter lilies?" At that moment the phone rang. "I'll get it, Mrs. Walters."

"Saint Bibiana's, Father Lucien here."

"Father, I'm sorry to bother you. This is Mother Mary Bernadette from Mount Saint Rita's. Is Father Erlich there by any chance?"

Lucien had been apprised by Detective Sullivan that they'd decided not to tell the good sisters the whole story of Erlich's disappearance. They didn't want to alarm them.

"He's not here right now, Mother. Could I take a message for him?"

"Yes, please. His sister has taken a turn for the worse. We were hoping he could come to see her."

"I'll make sure he gets the message when he returns. Would you like me to visit? I know her brother went every week and I'm sure it was a comfort to her."

"Oh, Father Erlich hasn't been here in quite some time," the nun informed him. "But you're certainly welcome to come. Please call us first. We'll keep you informed of her condition."

Lucien heard the phone click. He was curious as to why the pastor would lie about visiting his sister and what was even more of a mystery was where the man actually went every Wednesday. He called the police station to speak with Detective Sullivan who was not available.

"Please take a message to have him get in touch with Father Lucien. I need to talk to him as soon as possible."

He hung up the phone and called out to the secretary. "Mrs. Walters, does the name Effie sound familiar to you?"

She thought for a minute. "The only Effie I remember is Ephemia Fenner. You wouldn't remember her. It was right before they sent you here to help out. Miss Fenner was the nurse who took care of Father Erlich after his surgery. She lives in Massachusetts, now, I believe. I haven't heard her name in ages."

Lucien went next door to get the stick-it note from the back of the church directory.

༄

Stewart was in the kitchen when Kara arrived home. He was frosting an angel food cake. Her favorite. She gave him a hug. He helped her off with her jacket and pulled out a chair from the table for her to sit down. "How was your day?"

"I worked a few hours with Professor Hill at the forensics lab and spent time at the station going over the evidence from the Tucker case with Carl. We both agree the robbery at the church had been staged. We're not sure whether it was done to cover up the kidnapping of the priest or to cover up a theft by the priest."

"What does your instinct tell you?"

I think the he's still alive. Ruth gave me a tip he may have a gambling problem and Carl's decided to run a check on that. He and Sergeant Shwinnard went on a field trip to the casinos in Connecticut today."

"And they didn't ask you to tag along?"

"They did, but you know how I feel about those places. I realize they bring in a steady stream of income for the tribes and their investors, but the sight of those people sitting at the machines for hours sends shivers down my spine. So, for the sake of our daughter, I declined."

"Already an overprotective mother. I approve." He gave her a kiss as he placed a large slice of cake in front of her. "Please note the homemade fudge frosting. None of that canned stuff for my wife." He sat down across from her and poured them each a cup of tea.

"I met with Marjorie Tucker again today. At the azalea gardens."

"Was anything in bloom?"

"A few early daffodils and some snow flowers. Lots of buds, though. It's going to be beautiful in another month. You'll have to go with me."

"It's a date. And there'll be blooms in June and July, so we can bring the baby there for her first visit."

"I like that idea." She took out the picture of when she was younger and passed it on to her husband.

"I'm going to have to laminate this for you before it's totally worn to shreds," he said.

"Marjorie had photos of Anthony in the gardens. She shared them with me."

"That must have been difficult," he hesitated, "for both of you."

"I told her I'd find her son. I'm not sure I can keep my promise."

"I've never known you to say anything you didn't mean. If anyone can find out what happened to him, it will be you."

"Marjorie tried so hard to protect her child and yet, she lost him. She feels so guilty."

"Kara, you can't put children in protective bubble wrap. Our little girl will be fine. Don't worry."

"I can't help it. It's my job, I've seen how treacherous the world can be and I'm feeling overwhelmed by the responsibility of it all."

"But we'll be together and we can handle anything. And if we can't, we can always call in the heavy artillery."

"Gino and Sophia. Of course. What a good back-up plan. You're going to be an awesome dad."

"And you'll be a fantastic mom. Do you want another piece of cake?"

"Bring it on! I feel better already. And you can never have enough cake!"

10

Good Friday, March 30

Sullivan dealt with the paperwork on his desk, waiting until after eight to call the rectory.

"Father Lucien, this is Detective Sullivan. You left a message for me yesterday."

"Detective, I'm not sure if this will be of any help in finding Father Erlich but I spoke with one of the nuns at Mount St. Rita's where his sister is and she said they'd not seen him for quite awhile."

"They told us the same thing when we called to see if he might be there."

"Well, he led me to believe he went to visit his sister every week. He'd leave early Wednesday morning and didn't get back until late at night."

"Do you have any idea where he might have been going?"

"I'm not sure, but I may have a contact for you to call - a woman who once was his nurse. Effie."

It didn't take long to run a check on the telephone number he'd been given. The address was for an Ephemia Fenner in Attleboro, Massachusetts. He dialed the number and left a message on her phone he'd be stopping by in regard to a police matter. Then he phoned Kara.

"I think I may have a lead in the case. Do you feel like taking a ride?"

Sullivan stopped by the house to pick her up.

"Okay, what's this lead? Is it something you found out at Fox-woods?" she asked getting in the car.

"No, Foxwoods was a dead end, although one of the black jack dealers remembered a priest who came in regularly a few years back. He hasn't seen him there in a while. Shwinny won ten bucks, though. And I did buy some tickets for a show in July. It's a surprise for Jess's birthday."

"Then it wasn't a complete waste of time."

"I got this lead from Lucien, the young priest at St. Bib's. He found a number for someone from Erlich's past. A nurse. Ephemia Fenner." Sullivan explained the situation.

"So, Erlich has been lying about going to see his sister every week and you think this woman may have some information for us? Have you spoken with her?"

"I left a message but I don't want to wait until she gets back to me. The guy has no other relatives and no close friends. I'm hoping she can tell us something and I'd like you to ask the questions."

They parked in front of a 50s style ranch in a residential plat. The yard was well kept and two pink plastic flamingos greeted them on either side of the cement walkway. A woman in jeans and a royal blue Patriots sweatshirt answered the door. Sullivan introduced himself and Kara and she acknowledged she was, in fact, Ephemia Fenner. She glanced at the badge in Sullivan's right hand and turned her attention to the pregnant, black woman standing behind him at the bottom of the front steps.

"Please, come inside," she said, unlocking the screen door.

Sullivan stood aside and held the door open for Kara. A little boy with thick, dark curls, deep blue eyes, and a sprinkling of freckles across his nose sat on the floor watching television. He ran up to them and pointed to a Band Aid on his forehead. "I got stitches and I didn't even cry," he proudly announced.

"Sean fell and bumped his head last week," his mother explained.

"Father fixed. With holy water. I'm all better, now."

"You're a very brave young man," Kara told him and he nodded in complete agreement.

"Please have a seat." Effie motioned toward the couch. She turned off the television and sat in a chair by the window. The boy climbed up on her lap. The sunlight streaming in on his hair gave it an ebony sheen. His mother put her arms around him and he rested his head on her shoulder.

"Sean, this is Mr. Sullivan and Mrs. Langley."

"Hello." He waved at them from the safety of her arms. Kara waved back.

"I take it you're here in regard to the message you left on my phone this morning."

"We're investigating the disappearance of John Erlich and were hoping you could give us some information which might help us find him," Kara said.

"I took care of Father Erlich when I worked at South County Hospital. Right after he had his heart attack. I helped with his rehab. I moved out of Rhode Island several years ago. I like this area and it's not as remote as South Kingstown." She seemed to want to divert the conversation away from the priest. Kara decided to follow her lead.

"How long have you lived here?"

"I moved to this house four years ago, shortly before Sean was born."

"Are you still working?"

"I have a part-time job at a nursing home in the neighborhood. It's convenient because I can walk to work and I'm always nearby if my son needs me. I stayed home when he was first born." She brushed her hand over the boy's head. "When are you due?"

"In May. It's my first, so I'm sure I'll have to deal with work and raising a child. Like you do."

"It's not easy. I'm lucky, though. My mother helps with babysitting. Will you go back to work full time?"

"I've been putting in some hours at the forensics lab on campus. I'll definitely keep doing that. As for the police force, we haven't decided, yet."

"What does your husband do?"

"He teaches at the university. I'm sure he'll be a big help if I decide to go back to work full time. And your husband?"

"I'm a single mom."

"That must be hard on you."

"Yes, it has been." She turned her attention to the boy who was smiling up at her. "Would you like a snack?"

He jumped from her lap.

"I'll only be a minute. Can I offer either of you a drink?"

"No, thanks. We stopped at Dunkin Donuts on the way."

When they went into the kitchen, Kara got up to look at the photos hung on the wall. She stood in front of one and didn't turn from it when the woman came back into the room.

"This a nice picture of Father Erlich with you and your son."

"Yes, it was taken on the day he baptized Sean."

"Does he visit often?" Kara returned to the chair and sat down.

"He sometimes comes by on Wednesdays, my day off. He watches Sean so I can do some shopping and run errands. He's been a good friend to us."

"Was he here this Wednesday?"

The woman paused before answering. "No."

"Do you have any idea where he could be? I'm sure you're worried about him."

"He has no family, other than his sister and you must know she has Alzheimer's. He told me she doesn't even recognize him when he visits her."

"And you're not aware of any other friends he could be staying with?"

"No, no one. Father Erlich was a solitary individual. Other than us, young Father Lucien, and his parishioners, he didn't have any social contacts."

Sullivan stood up and gave her his card. "Thank you for your time, Ms. Fenner. I hope you'll be in touch should you hear from Father Erlich."

She walked them to the door and Kara placed a card in her hand before they left.

When they had pulled away from the curb, Sullivan said, "She's lying. She knows where he is. She's probably calling him right now."

"I'm sure she is," Kara agreed as she took out her cell phone and hit speed dial. "Sophia, it's Kara. Call me when you get off duty. I need you to find out information for me on a nurse who worked for a time at the hospital. Ephemia Fenner. Start with the cardiac unit. She took care of Father Erlich when he had his heart attack back in 2012."

"Well, we should know her whole life history by this afternoon now that Sophia's been recruited to help out."

"You can count on it," Kara assured him.

Sophia checked her phone messages in the cafeteria when she went on her break. The pediatric ward was having a quiet morning. She immediately went to a table where other nurses were chatting. It didn't take her long to find someone who remembered Effie.

"She'd been working on the cardiac wing for at least ten years by the time I started. She was a lot older than most of us, but really good at what she did. A workaholic," a young nurse explained.

"Was she married?" Sophia was curious.

"Not that I remember. She never spoke about anyone special in her life. She wasn't attractive and did nothing to make herself look pretty. But everyone loved her. She even worked extra hours doing rehab with the older patients. Mostly men, I think."

"Why did she leave the hospital?"

"She told us she had a better job offer and she wanted to live near her mother."

"Has anyone heard from her lately?"

"She wasn't close to anyone. However, there was a priest who was her patient and I remember him coming to the wards to give Communion and the Last Rites. An old guy. She took her breaks with him."

"Does he still visit here?"

"No, but I've talked to another priest who comes every so often. Father Lucien. He's cute. What a waste."

Sophia thanked her and returned to work. In the corridor outside the ward, she sat down and pulled out her cell phone.

"Kara, it's Sophia. I think you're on to something. It's possible those two are a couple. I'll do a little more snooping and stop by your place to fill you in on what I find out when my shift is over."

Gilbert sat waiting at the kitchen table for his wife to come home. He was hoping Darlene would bring him dinner. She and the girls had planned to do some shopping and then go for chowder and clam cakes at Iggy's Clam Shack in Point Judith to celebrate her birthday.

That afternoon, on the way home, he'd stopped at Patsy's Liquors and picked her up a bottle of peppermint schnapps she could share with them when they all came back to the house for a rousing game of mah-jong. He was looking forward to her bringing him home leftovers in one of those Styrofoam boxes. In all the years they'd been married, she'd never finished a meal at a restaurant. Not that they went out that often, although they had a yearly tradition of going out for breakfast the morning after her birthday to celebrate "a fresh new year of life," as she put it. He planned on taking her to the Coast Guard House in Narragansett this year. It was a bit fancier than in other years, but this was her sixtieth and he wanted to do something special. He'd told the hostess to reserve a table by the window so they could look out at the ocean while they ate. And he was going to hire a taxi to take them there. They would do it in style. He'd even bought a new tie for the occasion.

It was getting late and Gilbert was hungry. On Good Friday there was an excellent chance he'd find a tuna sandwich or two in the church refrigerator.

Above the altar, the crucifix was cloaked in a deep purple velveteen cloth to signify Jesus was dead. People were somber, coming in and out of the Sanctuary, lighting candles and saying prayers. A few elderly women were walking around the perimeter of the church doing the Stations of the Cross. He thought about making his confession and tallied up all the different sins he'd committed over the years. Kneeling at the altar rail, he grasped the rosary he'd finished making for Darlene that day. He managed to get through one Our Father, ten Hail Mary's, one Glory Be. Squeezing the beads into the gash the knife had reopened while he carved the crucifix, he imagined the pain Christ had felt on the cross - pain suffered for his sins. And the sadness came over him like a flow of molten lava. He pushed himself up from the kneeler and stumbled out of the Sanctuary into the church office.

Gilbert's head ached as he stood in front of the bathroom sink. He poured some whiskey over the throbbing cut and then drank straight from the bottle. He thought about taking the liquor with him. The priest wouldn't be missing it, since he was nowhere to be found.

He felt weak and sat on the couch until a wave of nausea passed. He hadn't had a seizure in years and this frightened him. *I need some air.* He tried to stand but couldn't lift himself. Slumped against the cushions, Gilbert let his mind wander. He made one last feeble attempt to rise. *I have to get home to Darlene. I haven't wished her a happy birthday.*

"Gilbert, I'm home." Darlene called down the stairs. A light was on and she thought she could hear the radio's static. "I guess he's fallen asleep," she said to the women settling in around the kitchen table. "I'll put these leftovers into the fridge and get out the cookies - Pepperidge Farm classic assortment. And look." She brought the schnapps to the table. "My husband never forgets my birthday," she said proudly. "He's taking me out for breakfast tomorrow. I going to wear my new fascinator."

They opened the cookie tin, poured the liquor, and raised their glasses in a toast of appreciation. "To Gilbey!" they shouted. Doreen put out her foot and kicked the cellar door. "I'll just close this so we don't wake him up."

11

Saturday, March 31

Sergeant Shwinnard came into the station earlier than usual. The dispatcher met him in the corridor outside his office.

"There's a woman sitting on the bench in the hall. A Mrs. Cheevers. She mentioned we've been trying to get in touch with her husband. She'd like to talk with you."

"Send her right in, Leo." He waited at the door to escort her in. "Have a seat, Mrs. Cheevers. Lovely, ummmm, hat you have there," he said.

"Thank you, Sergeant." She pushed the veil from her forehead and a purple feather from a tiny finch dislodged and floated onto his desk. "It's a fascinator."

"That it is, indeed, Ma'am!" He handed the feather to her and waited while she tucked it back under the nest and the olive satin ribbon, which seemed to be tentatively holding the entire creation together.

"And what can I do for you this fine morning?"

"Well, I was hoping you could help me locate my husband." She took a photo from her bag and handed it to him. "You may have noticed him on your daily rounds - wandering around Peace Dale. He's gone missing. You see, he was supposed to take me out to breakfast – to celebrate my forty-fourth birthday. But he's nowhere to be found."

Shwinnard hid his surprise well. She had to be sixty, if she was a day. "Congratulations, my dear. But you mentioned he's been known to wander around the neighborhood. Perhaps he woke up early and will be returning soon?"

"Oh, no, Sergeant. One thing my Gilbert is, is reliable. If he says he's going to do a thing, he does it. He always takes me out the day after my birthday. When I'm a full day older. It's a date. We've been doing it for the past thirty years."

Shwinnard did the math which would have made her fourteen when she married, but he kept his subtracting skills to himself. "We'll see what we can do, Ma'am. I'll have one of my patrolmen scour the neighborhood. Does he have any friends or neighbors he likes to visit?"

"Not that I know of, but he's very religious and is a regular church-goer. We've belonged to St. Bibiana's since we were married there in 1982."

Shwinnard stopped himself from doing the math and helped her out of her seat. "I'll be in touch if we catch sight of him and please call us if he does come home."

He walked the child bride to her car, wishing her a Happy Birthday and then decided to go for a quick drive around the village.

Sullivan checked his messages first thing when he arrived at work. Nothing yet from Father Erlich. Kara and he had taken odds on how long it would take the priest to get in touch. The man certainly wouldn't want them going back to the house to question Effie again. Kara thought it would be soon.

"He'll need time to concoct a good story," she said to Sullivan when she'd called him at home on Friday evening to share what she'd learned from Sophia.

"What you found out pretty much confirms the two were good friends, if not more. What do you figure? Will he show his face today or wait 'til next week?" Sullivan asked.

I'm guessing he'll resurrect tomorrow," she said. "If you don't hear from him by the end of today, send Sergeant Shwinnard to St. Bib's for Mass."

"I'll make sure I do that," he assured her. "Happy Easter."

He went in search of Shwinnard. "Leo, have you seen the Sarge today?"

"He was here earlier and met with a Mrs. Cheevers. She came in to report her husband missing. I think he's out looking for him."

"Tell him to see me when he shows up."

A few minutes later Leo buzzed in to tell him a Mr. Maxwell Jacques was on the other line wanting to speak to him about his wife, Minerva. "It appears she's gone missing, too, Sir. Seems like Peace Dale has turned into a regular black hole," Leo commented as he transferred the call into the office.

He listened to the details and informed Jacques he could come in to file a missing person's report after his wife had been gone for forty-eight hours.

Maxwell explained it was really the Buick he was concerned about. "It's not in the garage. There's some equipment I need in the trunk."

Sullivan jotted down the license plate number and promised to notify him if the car was sighted.

Maxwell was looking through the telephone numbers in her address book an hour later when she walked into her bedroom.

"What are you doing going through my dresser?" Minnie rushed forward to slam the drawer shut. She was worried he'd found the expensive cashmere sweaters and the necklace she'd bought with his charge card and hidden away with the other items she had stashed in her bureau.

"Minerva, you startled me. Where have you been?"

"I told you I was going shopping. I had things to do."

"That was yesterday, Minerva! You know I have a rehearsal this afternoon."

She grabbed the book from his hands. "What does your rehearsal have to do with me, Maxwell?"

"You took my car. The lighting board from church is in the trunk!" He looked at her disgustedly and placed a call to the station. "This is Maxwell Jacques. I'm sorry to bother you again but my wife has been found."

In the background Leo heard a woman's voice yelling, "I was never lost, you fool!"

❧

Today was the day Ruth was going to do the final stage blocking and Samuel and Clay were bringing in the last set pieces and putting them in place. She did a double take, suddenly recognizing the chairs, tables, and sideboard the crew was hauling on to the stage.

"Is there any furniture left in Arthur's dining room?"

"He eats in his study, in front of the TV- which, I might add, we left right where it was. He'll never even notice anything's missing," Samuel said as he went back outside to where Clovis and Reggie struggled to take the larger pieces out of the truck.

"Where is Arthur, anyway?" she asked Clay who was busy placing newspapers and magazines on the side tables.

"He went to the Village Barbershop to get a haircut and then had a hot date with a lady we introduced him to. He'll be here in time for rehearsal."

Samuel came back inside calling out directions to Reggie and Clovis on where to situate the Victorian sofa.

"Did you two, by any chance, arrange for this date to get Arthur out of the house?" Ruth asked, already knowing the answer to her question.

"Gotta go organize the props table," Samuel muttered pulling Clay with him backstage behind the safety of the curtain.

"Wow! The set looks great." Kara gave Ruth a thumbs-up and sat next to her on the couch. She took out her notebook and put it on the end table. "Hey, this stuff looks vaguely familiar. Doesn't Arthur have a throw pillow exactly like this?"

"Good detecting skills there, Sherlock," Ruth said. "I wonder how long it will take him to catch on that his two best friends have emptied out his house?"

Kara laughed. "It's amazing how much mischief those two can stir up."

They went over the blocking together as the cast began to assemble in the auditorium.

Gino and Rick had finished painting the flats and were busy helping to hang the Fresnel's according to the lighting plan Maxwell had given Ruth. He hadn't arrived yet, but the two brothers knew what they were doing, so work was being accomplished. Sophia was arranging the costumes in a wardrobe off stage right. With only two weeks left, it looked like the show would definitely be ready on time.

"I'm going to need a roll of silver duct tape to mark some of the key positions on the stage," she called to the stage crew manager who pulled out a package from his toolbox.

"Hey, give this to Ruth," he yelled, throwing the tape at one of the guys standing on the edge of the stage.

The actor playing Christopher reached out to catch it and lost his balance, falling off the apron and crashing onto the floor below. Gino and Rick rushed over to help him up.

"I'm okay. No harm done," he announced. But as he started to move back to the stage, he yelped out in pain.

Sophia sat him on the stairs and examined his leg. "I think he may have broken his ankle. Gino, let's get him to the emergency room." They stood on either side helping him hobble out to the parking lot.

"There goes my main character," Ruth muttered to her husband. "This play truly is cursed. I think it's time to throw in the towel."

"We've gotten this far and I'm sure this is simply another small obstacle to overcome," Kara declared. "We'll use one of the stand-ins. Clovis, come over here. You are now our new Christopher Wren."

Clovis looked around at the rest of the cast in shock as Reggie gave him a high five.

"I'm not sure I can be ready. I've never been very good at memorizing," he admitted.

Kara patted him on the back. "You'll be fine. I'll work with you." She handed him a script. "Here, start studying."

"See, Kara to the rescue - problem solved," Rick gave his wife a kiss. "The show will go on."

"It's like she's a tall, black, female Mickey Rooney," Arthur whispered admiringly in Samuel's ear.

"Mickey Rooney! You two old coots are really showing your age," Clay chuckled.

"*Babes on Broadway* with Judy Garland," Arthur said wistfully. "Busby Berkeley musicals - my mother loved them. She considered Berkeley the most famous film director ever. They sure don't make shows like they used to."

"Amen!" they all agreed.

"Enough with the praying. Could someone help me carry this lighting equipment inside? Unless one of you has heavenly powers and can levitate it into the building?" Maxwell had arrived and it was time to get back to work.

᷈

12

EASTER SUNDAY, APRIL 1

Saint Bibiana's was crowded for the morning's Easter Service. During the past two weeks, a feeling of peace had descended over the church and today, many parishioners had assembled for worship because word was out the young priest would be celebrating Mass.

The traditional violet veiling had been removed from the crucifix and statues. Sunlight streamed through the stained glass windows casting wavering shades of red, yellow and deep blue over the churchgoers. Everyone stood as Father Lucien and the altar servers entered together and the choir sang out:

The grave now is empty!
The stone is rolled away!
Hallelujah!
Happy Resurrection Day!

From a bench in the balcony, Sergeant Shwinnard observed the people below, recognizing some he'd interviewed in the course of their search for the missing pastor. He was keeping himself entertained by trying to count the fascinators on the women in the pews. The purple and olive green one was nowhere to be seen.

When Father Lucien began his sermon, he gazed out upon those he was beginning to think of as his flock. Smiling faces looked up at him as he spoke of forgiveness and triumph over evil and quoted Saint Peter's words of "new birth into a living hope". After the sermon, and the offertory, he prepared to serve Communion and was beginning the *Agnus Dei* when he suddenly stopped ringing the bell, imagining he'd heard a voice calling out to him.

From the left side of the church, Shwinnard noticed a slight stirring, as people seemed to be looking toward the confessional, nudging each other. Their whispers mingled with soft moans coming from inside the booth. A woman on the end of the pew closest to the box got up to peek inside. The door swung open. A cloaked figure stumbled out and began staggering toward the altar. The woman clutched at her heart, screaming and grasping at the arms of the people closest to her.

Father Lucien stopped what he was doing and hurried from the altar as Shwinnard moved quickly to get to the frantic scene now taking place below. The figure had reached the front and fallen prostrate at the bank of votive candles. Using the altar rail to pull himself up, he shed the velvet draping and turned slowly to face the congregation.

A teenager in one of the pews asked loudly, "Is this an April Fool's joke?" His mother shushed the boy. The parishioners were transfixed by the drama taking place in front of them. Shwinnard and Father Lucien followed to catch up with the man as he ran from the Sanctuary.

The young priest soon returned to reassure the flustered members of his flock and to finish the service.

Standing over the figure now seated at the desk in the church office, the sergeant phoned Detective Sullivan. "Carl, this is Shwinnard. I'm at Saint Bib's. Your hunch was right. Father Erlich is officially back among the living."

The priest sat sipping Communion wine from a paper cup. He appeared to be dazed. The sergeant didn't intend to start questioning the pastor until Sullivan had shown up.

"Can you go to the kitchen to get me something to eat? I don't like drinking on an empty stomach. There's usually something in the refrigerator or the cupboard next to the sink."

"I'll do that for you as soon as Detective Sullivan arrives. He's on his way."

Shwinnard wanted to make sure he kept the priest under his watchful eye. He sat across from him and they waited in silence until the door opened. Only then did he leave the room to go in search of food.

"Father Erlich. I'm Police Detective Carl Sullivan. It's good you're back home. We've been looking for you. We've got a few questions. But first I need to know if you require a doctor."

"A doctor? I don't want a doctor."

"You appear a bit groggy, Father. Have you been hurt?"

"I'm fine. I just have a headache." Shwinnard returned and handed the priest a piece of bread. He bit into the slice and chewed on it for a minute before swallowing.

"I think you should let us take you to the hospital."

The priest held up his right hand. "No!" He took another bite.

"Can you tell us where you've been for the past two weeks?"

"I think you already know that, Detective." Erlich looked at him expectantly and put the bread down on the desk.

"How did you manage to get up to Massachusetts, Father? Your car is still at the rectory."

"Effie picked me up."

"And you've been with her all this time?"

"Yes."

"Why didn't you call someone to let them know you were all right?"

"Because I wasn't all right."

Sullivan and Shwinnard waited for him to explain but the priest picked up the bread and put the rest of it into his mouth. He took a gulp of wine and swallowed hard before he continued. "I was far from all right. I had a breakdown and Effie came and brought me home with her."

"Father, church funds were missing from the office. Did you take the money with you?"

"Yes, I wasn't thinking straight at the time. I tried to give it to Effie for taking care of me. But she wouldn't have it. I returned it to the safe when I came back to the office last night."

"You were here yesterday?"

"Effie dropped me off at the church. It was late. I had a key to the side door in the basement. I came to the office to put the money back in the safe. I sat at my desk and thought about what I was going to say. How I was going to explain my actions to Father Lucien? To the congregation?"

He took out a silver flask from his jacket pocket and gave it to Sullivan. He opened it up, sniffed, and handed it back to Shwinnard.

"Irish whiskey. I keep it in a mouthwash bottle in the medicine chest for refills." He pointed to the bathroom behind him. "I had a few swigs to give me some Dutch courage. I was really tired and put my head down. I think I fell asleep. Someone put a cloth around me, like a shroud. And I remember a voice or voices asking if I would hear their confessions. It could have been a dream, but I think someone helped me into the Sanctuary. Into the confessional. That's the last thing I remember until this morning."

"We're going to need to have the contents examined." Sullivan pulled Shwinnard aside. "And check the inventory of the office and bathroom we recorded the day of the robbery. I remember a full Listerine bottle being on the list. Go see if it's still in the chest."

Shwinnard returned and pulled Sullivan aside. "The bottle's still there where we left it. But now it's almost empty."

Ruth and Rick were hosting a Sunday brunch and, as usual, everyone was lending a hand. Stewart was in the kitchen showing Sophia how to make his famous Easter Eggs Benedict with crushed jellybeans mixed into the Hollandaise sauce. Kara had brought along hot cross buns for those who were looking for a more traditional choice. Rick was flipping johnnycakes and frying bacon on the grill while Ruth and Gino were setting the table in the dining room.

"I invited the boys. Arthur may be bringing along a date, so be nice," Ruth warned Gino who had just finished licking the sugar cross off the top of one of the pastries. He popped the whole thing in his mouth.

"Whasatsposetamean?" He took another bun from the platter. She gave him a wary look.

Kara asked, "Is that the woman the guys had fixed him up with so they could empty out his house while they were on a date?"

"Yup. Clay knows her from some of the concerts he's directed. She's in the South County Singers. I invited him and Samuel, too. They should be here by now."

They heard a car pull up into the driveway. Kara looked out. "Well the three amigos are here, but no girlfriend - I mean, woman friend."

"They're probably really hungry." Gino went to the door and handed each one a hot cross bun as they entered.

Samuel patted him on the back and teased, "Thanks, man. Are you rehearsing for the role of ticket-taker?"

Not getting a part in the play was still a sore spot for Gino, so he snatched the pastry from Samuel and popped it into his own mouth.

Arthur threw himself down in an armchair in front of the fireplace. "Must be nice to have furniture," he said, looking directly at Samuel who decided to retreat into the safety of the kitchen.

"Whew, it's rough out there. I'll just help you in here," he told Rick.

"Where is your new friend?" Ruth asked Arthur as they finished setting the table.

"Due to a series of unfortunate events, Lynette will not be joining us today," he announced.

"The poor woman had a traumatic experience at Mass this morning. A man in a purple blanket jumped out at her from the confessional during the service. It scared the bejesus out of her. She's got a heart condition. They took her to the hospital to have her checked out," Clay said.

Everyone in the room immediately stopped what they were doing and gawked at Arthur and Clay, waiting for either of the men to elaborate on what they'd said. Kara finally broke the silence. "And who was this mysterious, cloaked figure?"

"It was the missing priest. Father Erlich."

"He's not dead?" Sophia asked.

"Nope, he's still alive. Resurrected this morning during Mass," Samuel explained coming out from the kitchen with another platter of hot cross buns.

"Hey, dat's a good one. Easter - dead guy - resurrection," Gino took a warm bun from the platter and presented it to Samuel. He appeared to be the only one in the group who appreciated the humor. Everyone else stood stunned at the latest news.

Sophia said aloud what they were all thinking. "Let's get this food on the table. It's only a matter of time before Kara gets a call."

Right on cue, the buzz of a cell phone interrupted their conversation.

They watched as Kara answered. "Hello, Carl ... Yes, I heard. I'll be right there."

Lynnette Stritch told her story to the nice lady detective who was sitting with her in the Emergency Room. She'd brought her a cup of hot tea. Lynnette felt safer here. She hadn't come across too many policewomen. She suspected they must have to work harder than the men to get to the rank of detective and speculated if taking maternity leave could potentially jeopardize their job status. She wondered how many months pregnant the woman was and if she intended to have the baby at work in the Safety Complex rather than risk a few days away from her desk. It was probably as good a place as any. The detective broke into her thoughts and Lynnette focused on the soft, calming voice.

"Mrs. Stritch, are you feeling better?"

"Yes. My heart has stopped pounding."

"About what time do you think it was when you first heard noises, Mrs. Stritch?"

"10:22. I'd just checked my FitBit. It was a birthday present from my son. The moaning got louder. I opened the door a tad and looked inside. It was dark. Then a figure jumped up and clawed at my hand. I pulled away and screamed. It came at me, covered with the purple cloth they drape over the statues of Mary and the saints to remind us of Jesus's sacrifice." She took a sip of tea and closed her eyes. "At first I thought it might be Gilbert."

"Gilbert Cheevers?"

"Yes, his wife Darlene is a friend of mine. She said he's gone missing."

"Why would you think it was him, Mrs. Stritch?"

"He likes to listen in on confessions, you know. And I'm almost sure I saw him Friday night in church. The night he disappeared. I was making the Stations of the Cross and he was kneeling up at the altar."

"Are you're sure it was him?"

"Yes, positive. He walks around the village and shops at the Jonny-cake Center each Thursday, like clockwork, when the new donations come in for us to sort. There's a group of women who volunteer to go through the merchandise before it's priced and put out for the customers."

"Did you speak with him on Friday?"

"Oh, no. I never speak with anyone on Good Friday. I've always observed the silence since I was a young child. Most Catholics who follow the old practice keep silent from 12-3, but I don't say a word from the time I get up on Friday until I rise on Saturday morning."

"What was Mr. Cheevers doing when you saw him?"

"He was kneeling at the altar saying the rosary. I saw him get up and head out toward the office. He seemed quite unsteady. I was going to ask him if he needed help, but someone followed him and I assumed he was going to take care of it."

"It was a man? Did you recognize him?"

"No, I was too far away. I thought it was a man. Whoever it was wore a dark coat with a hood. Now, come to think of it, I'm not so sure."

"Thank you, Mrs. Stritch. This must have been a shock for you and I'm sorry you had to relive it again, but I promise you can go home soon."

"It was," she teared up. "I kept screaming at the top of my lungs and finally the nice sergeant took my arm and brought me into the back sitting room. They sent for an ambulance and brought me here. I don't think I have anything else to add," she said apologetically to Kara.

"You've been a great help. We'll be in touch if we have any more questions. Here's my card. I had them call your son and he should be here soon to take you home."

Kara was waiting for Sullivan in his office. He sat in the chair next to her. "I'm sorry to keep bothering you, but I really need your help. How is Mrs. Stritch?"

"She's fine. I stayed until her son arrived. She didn't have much to offer about how Erlich came to be in the confessional, but something came up about that missing person's case Sergeant Shwinnard's working on."

"You mean Cheevers?"

"She told me she saw him in church on Friday night. He was saying the rosary and appeared to be ill. She said someone followed him out the back of the Sanctuary."

"We'll check on that. One case solved and another case opened."

"I can't help but think they're connected in some way. So, what did Erlich have to say?"

"His story is he was in his office and got a call from Ephemia Fenner. Something must have upset him because he told her to come and get him. He went to the rectory and waited until she arrived. He states he was at her house the whole time."

"No foul play was involved?"

"Nothing he wanted to share."

"Has anyone questioned the pastor about confessions he's heard?"

"Shwinnard had already checked with Erlich who told him it was none of his business what went on between a confessor and a penitent and anyways, he hadn't listened to anything out of the ordinary. 'Just a bunch of old women who have nothing juicy to confess', in the priest's own words."

"So, Erlich didn't leave the church on Saturday because he was in danger?"

"Apparently not. He said he had been having a crisis of faith and had to get away."

"Do you believe him?"

"I don't know. He's a man with a lot of secrets, if you ask me."

"I'll speak with Ephemia Fenner again and get her take on the situation. I think she'll tell me the truth."

When she arrived, Effie was in the front yard playing tag with Sean, catching him and holding him high above her head listening to his laughter. She didn't seem surprised to see the woman detective again. She put the little boy safely down and he ran up to Kara and tagged her. "You're it!" Kara took a small plush rabbit from her pocket and gave it to him.

"Happy Easter, Sean."

"Mommy, mine?" He showed his mother the present.

"Yes, you can keep it. What do you say?"

"Thank you." He shook Kara's hand.

"You're welcome."

Sean ran to his wagon and began to pull the bunny around in it. The two women sat down in the webbed lawn chairs facing one another.

"I'm sorry I didn't tell you the truth. I don't like lying. I'm not very good at it."

"No, you're not. We realized he'd come back as soon as he found out we'd been to see you. He seems to care deeply for you and Sean."

She looked searchingly at the woman whose head was bowed to avoid making eye contact.

"He's a wonderful man. I thank God every day he's in our lives."

Kara let her silence fill the air around them.

"You know, don't you?"

"Yes."

"How?"

"The baptism photo. The way he's holding the baby - looking so lovingly at him ... It can't be easy for any of you."

"I'd never ask him to leave the priesthood. But, it's been tough for us."

"You mentioned your mother. Is there anyone else to help you?"

"My sister and her family want nothing to do with me. The last time we spoke she reminded me we're black and we were brought up to be God-fearing Baptists. Having an illegitimate child by a white, Catholic priest puts me in the same category with Jezebel. I've committed the ultimate sin in their eyes."

Kara let that settle over them.

"How is he? I didn't want him to go back. He's not well. But John told me about the church funds. He explained he'd only borrowed them to make money for us. He's gambled before and won. He gave me the down payment for this house. And he had a great cover -no one at the casino would ever think a priest would be good at counting cards. I refused to take any of the money and insisted he had to return it immediately."

"He counted cards?"

"It's something his older sister taught him when he was a boy. You wouldn't know, looking at her now, but she had a photographic memory. They were both smart kids. Unfortunately it was their older brother who was educated. John told me it's how it was back then in Irish households. Any money was invested in the eldest son. When their father died in an accident at the mill, the insurance money went to cover Joe's college tuition. Such a waste."

"Why do you say that?"

"His brother wasn't very smart. Not like Gervase and John. And like his dad, Joe drank. He wasn't out of college a month when he left a party and walked across a street in downtown Boston. He got run over by a tour bus. Within a year their mother had died, too – of a broken heart, John said. His sister went in the convent and the parish priest found a place for him in a seminary in Peace Dale."

"Was he ever happy?"

"He says he was in the beginning. They gave him a good education and the parishes he was assigned to were appreciative. He had stature. People looked up to him. It wasn't until much later that he began to question the choices he'd made. I believe he always yearned for his own family. He said he would visit his parishioners and wish sometimes he didn't have to go home to his tiny cell in the rectory. He was always a man torn between two worlds."

"And then there was you and Sean."

"Still a man torn between two worlds."

"Did you know him before his heart attack?"

"I knew of him. He wasn't well liked from what I'd heard. But he was my patient and this was a very different relationship than pastor and parishioner. He was facing his own mortality and he became dependent on me for comfort. For the first time, he was not the one responsible for everyone else. I think the helplessness of it all made him look at the world in a different light."

"He began to question?"

"He became unsure. Fearful of everything. He didn't want to leave the hospital. He felt he was safe only when I was with him. It was a terrible time for him. But he never questioned his faith. I knew he wouldn't leave the church for me. But then, as you said, there was Sean and, well, you can imagine." They looked at the little boy pulling his wagon around the yard collecting grey stones and yellow dandelions. "He'd still be here if I hadn't told him about your visit."

"When did you drop him off at church?"

"He came home late on Friday and was upset when he heard you and Detective Sullivan knew about me. We talked all day Saturday and he decided he had to go back. Sean was asleep. We put him in the car and I drove John to the church. It was late - around 10:30. The building was in darkness. I knew something must have been wrong later because he told me to call his cell when I got home. He wanted to know we were safe. But when I did phone, he didn't answer. I was so worried. Thank you for calling me … Will he go to jail?"

"I don't think so. He's returned the money and, as of yet, no charges have been filed against him. I don't know about his situation in the church, however. The hierarchy tends to frown on priests having families."

"Will you inform the bishop John has a family?"

"I'll share this information with Detective Sullivan. He'd have had to arrest him if charges were pressed but ultimately it's John's decision what to do about his personal situation. I think the two of you need to have a serious discussion about what is best for all of you, especially Sean."

"Thank you. This has been such a nightmare. But sometimes things happen for the best. Maybe it will force us to finally make some difficult choices."

Kara stood up to leave and the little boy stopped playing and hugged the bunny. "I hope it all works out well for you. You deserve to be happy together. Call me if you need anything or if you just want to have lunch."

The little boy smiled up at Kara and put the bunny close to his heart.

She got into her car and waved at the mother and son. She'd wanted to ask Effie about six years ago when the couple had first met. She wanted to find out if the woman knew anything about Anthony Tucker's disappearance. But she'd learned enough today and decided to leave those questions for another time.

～

APRIL

From you have I been absent in the spring,
When proud-pied April, dressed in all his trim,
Hath put a spirit of youth in everything,
That heavy Saturn laughed and leaped with him.

Sonnet 98, William Shakespeare

April is the cruelest month, breeding
Lilacs out of the dead land, mixing
Memory and desire, stirring
Dull roots with spring rain.

The Waste Land, T. S. Eliot

13

MONDAY, APRIL 2

He woke up in the dark and dressed in the bathroom so as not to wake Jess. Then he paused in the hall to look in on his sons who were still sleeping peacefully. Max was curled up at the foot of Billy's bed. His ears twitched but the puppy didn't move from the quiet comfort of the boys' room.

Next week was the beginning of school vacation and Carl had promised he'd take the family on an adventure. He never made promises he couldn't keep, but he wondered, now, if he'd have even a minute to spare in the coming days. One mystery traded for another. So many strands to connect. He was confident he was a good detective, but this was more than he'd expected when he agreed to step into the job last fall.

He left the house as the sun was rising. They'd had made plans for an early meeting when Kara called to tell him about her conversation with Ms. Fenner. The priest's story was corroborated, but it still did not account for his whereabouts on Friday when Cheevers was last seen at the church. Fenner implied the priest was at the casino nearby in Lincoln.

The team sat around the conference table with notebooks, laptops and folders spread out in front of them. Sergeant Shwinnard stood at an easel with a flip pad to jot down anything of significance while they reviewed their notes out loud. As they brainstormed, he created a summary of the critical events in chronological order.

Saturday night, March 17 - Erlich reported missing. Last seen going to his office at church on Saturday afternoon, office in disarray, money missing from the vault.

Sunday, March 18 to Saturday, March 31 - Investigation launched. Parishioners and people connected with priest are questioned. He's disliked but no one has reason to harm him. Team follows leads:

1. Gambling in Connecticut – blackjack dealer recognizes him but has not seen him lately.

2. Erlich's sister Gervase, a nun, has late stage Alzheimer's. Tells Lucien he visits her in Cumberland every Wednesday but Mother Superior says he hasn't been to see her in weeks.

3. Ephemia Fenner, a nurse who cared for him after his heart attack 6 years ago. He is staying with her and her son. Interview with Ephemia results in Erlich coming to church on Saturday night to return "borrowed" money to safe.

Sunday, April 1 – Erlich suddenly appears in church during Easter service.

1. He's dazed and tells them he doesn't know how he got into the confessional.

2. He thinks someone led him there the night before. Drugs were found mixed in the whiskey in the mouthwash bottle which he used to refill the flask.

3. Explains his disappearance on a "Crisis of Faith." Possible panic attack. Called Ephemia Fenner for help. She picked him up on Saturday afternoon, March 17, and brought him to her home in Massachusetts, returning him to the church two weeks later on Saturday night, March 31.

4. Fenner corroborates his story.

Detective Brown added that he'd spoken with the diocese administrator and it appeared no charges were being brought against Erlich seeing as he'd returned the borrowed money with interest earned from gambling at a casino in northern RI. "They prefer keeping the matter quiet and his bishop will be conferring with him this week. Until then,

Father Lucien will be in charge and continue as he has during the last two weeks. Erlich is lying low in the rectory, not speaking with anyone except Lucien."

Sullivan turned to Kara, "Did you learn anything else when you spoke with Miss Fenner yesterday?"

Kara hesitated. She'd filled Carl in on most of the conversation and he was aware she didn't want to share what she'd been told in confidence with the others in the room. "Ephemia gave me some background on Erlich, but nothing relating to this case except his motive for disappearing. She agreed he was having issues regarding his vocation and needed time to think about what he intended to do in the future. I'd like to speak with him today. Maybe he'll give me a clearer picture of what's going on in his head?"

Carl's cell phone rang, and he stepped outside the room returning a few minutes later. "Mrs. Cheevers called to say her husband still has not returned home."

"So, this case remains open," Detective Brown said.

Kara agreed wholeheartedly with his assessment. "Wide open!"

Mrs. Brody came to the door wearing an apron, its kangaroo pockets stuffed with brushes and rags, a squeegee and a Windex bottle. "Ah, good mornin to ya, darlin. Come on in and take a load off yer feet. I put ta kettle on right after ye called. I'm glad yer here. He's not been this upset since the little boy got hurt the day he had his heart attack." She led Kara to the couch. The coffee table was set with a polished silver tea service, white linen napkins, and some Irish biscuits on a plate decorated with green shamrocks outlined in gold. "Let me jest pour you a cuppa. Ah, there ye are, Father. Mizz Langley's come by to sit a spell with ye. I'll jest be goin back ta my spring cleanin. Call if ye be needin anythin I'll jest be outside finishin the windas. Got ta make sure the sunshine can get in, now, dontcha know it."

"Thank you, Mrs. Brody," Kara took the cup . The priest waited until the back door slammed, then lowered himself wearily into the well-worn chair across from the couch.

Kara put a teaspoon of sugar into her tea and stirred it slowly. She pushed the sugar bowl toward him.

"I prefer mine with cream. Mrs. Brody makes a strong brew." He took a sip from the cup and put it on the highly polished end table next to him, being careful to place a lace doily underneath. "Detective Langley, I thought you might be paying me a visit. Effie called to tell me you'd spent time with her and the boy yesterday. She said she felt better after talking with you. She told me she thought you'd make an excellent priest. Said you're a good listener."

Kara smiled at him. "We both have jobs requiring us to pay careful attention to what people say. And don't say."

"Effie believes I can trust you and I respect her opinion on people. She's a wonderful person. Whenever I felt like I was drowning, she's been there to bring me back to shore. I don't know if she can save me this time." His hand shook as he picked up the cup. Some of the liquid dripped on to the table. Kara took the napkin, rose from the couch, and blotted up the spill. She placed her hand on his shoulder.

"Maybe this time you're strong enough to make it to the shore on your own?"

"I've been a priest almost my whole life. It's what I chose to be. I don't know anything else. I've memorized all the prayers, and the rules, and the rites. They're written down if I should ever forget. I only need to go the appropriate book, the appropriate page, and there it is. Why I'm here. What I am expected to believe. How I'm expected to act. And if I don't find an answer there, I can always call on my faith to lead me down the right path. No questions necessary. My blind faith shall lead me safely to some distant shore - up from the waters of Babylon."

A tune from her mother's favorite hymn ran through Kara's head as she sat back down. *Shall we gather at the river, the beautiful, the beautiful river.*

"I worry I won't be able to provide for them. That I'll be a burden. I'm old. But they're so alone and I watch the two of them together and I want to protect my son from all the terrible things the world throws at us." He put his hands together as if in prayer, then continued.

"When Effie called and told me Sean had fallen in the playground and she'd taken him to the hospital, I felt so helpless. I should have been there for him. And I was angry at the person who should have been taking care of the boy. He's so little. He can't take care of himself. Adults are supposed to keep children away from danger, away from harm. I can't emphasize this enough with my church school teachers. I'd been working on a sermon about that very topic when she called. When she hung up, I rose from my chair. I was in a rage. I threw things. I took the money from the safe and called Effie to come and get me. I'd made up my mind. I was done with all of it. People unburdening their troubles, their sins on me. Who was I, a wretched sinner myself, to grant them pardon? I felt free. I didn't think of the repercussions. I just needed to be with them. To keep them safe." He buried his face in his hands and his shoulders silently heaved.

Kara sat rigid. The priest had said everything she herself had been dealing with after walking out of her office last August and since she learned she was going to have a child. She remembered the young woman, Blaine, who had died on her watch. And of Anthony. "I kept him close to me. I thought I was keeping him safe, but I lost him." All Kara's deeply hidden fears now felt raw and exposed as she placed both hands on her stomach, linking her fingers tightly.

"I'm sorry to burden you with all of this. I have no one else to tell."

"What do you suppose you'll do, Father?"

"I don't know. I don't think there is a chapter or verse which will guide me through this and what faith I had has been sorely tried. I honestly don't know."

There was silence between them until the sound of the kitchen door opened and shut, followed by the housekeeper coming into the room.

"Kin I freshen up yer tea for ye a bit?"

"Thank you, Mrs. Brody, but I have to get on to work now."

The housekeeper gathered the cups and took the tea tray into the kitchen.

"Will you come back to talk again, Detective?" Erlich asked.

"I will."

He escorted her to the front door. Kara turned to him. "I wish you peace in whatever your decision is, Father. Please give Effie and Sean my regards when you speak with them."

The campus was busy and Kara decided to park in the police headquarters across from Fogarty Hall where she was working in the state forensics lab. She'd been bothered by something mentioned in passing and sat for a few minutes in her car before calling the station.

"Leo, it's Detective Langley. Would you move the Tucker files into my office? I'm at URI right now but I'll be back to go over them again. Thanks."

Professor Hill was standing over a table in the trace evidence lab. "Good morning, Kara. I've been working diligently and can confirm there was a sedative in the whiskey the priest drank." He held up the mouthwash bottle. "Quite a lot of it. Enough to knock him out for a few hours at least."

"Then someone could have brought him to the confessional like he said."

"But how would they know ahead of time the priest was going to be in the church that night?" Hill asked.

"I haven't worked it through yet. Unless he had plans to meet someone there?"

"You could check his cell phone to see if a call was made and to whom."

"The good father says his phone has disappeared. It was one of those disposable models you get at Job Lot. He had it with him when he arrived at the church but can't find it. I'm sure he's hiding something from us. I need to follow up on a few leads to see if I'm right."

"And what about the guy who disappeared from church the night before?"

"Gilbert Cheevers."

"Yeah, that guy. What if he put the sedative in the whiskey? Or what if it was put there knowing Cheevers would drink it?"

"Why do you say that, Professor?"

"I have some trace evidence from the church I'd like you to look at. It was found under the couch cushion in the church office." He took out gloves for them both to put on and brought out a crushed black and red bead. "Be careful when you handle this. It's lethal if it gets into your blood stream because it has potent effects on protein synthesis." He handed her a pair of latex gloves.

Kara pushed the bead around with her index finger. "What is it?"

"It's called a rosary pea. *Abrus precatorius* from the bean family, *Fabaceae*. It grows wild down in Florida and is even found here in the Northeast. Women in Peru use it to make jewelry. They know to be very careful when they're stringing the beads together. You could swallow one whole and not be affected as long as the outer shell is not broken. The poison inside is called anbrim. It's actually more dangerous than ricin."

"Wow! What are the effects if anbrim does get into the system?"

"Nausea, seizures, kidney failure, and finally death. If Cheevers handled this bead on Friday and it entered his blood stream, he is certainly dead somewhere."

"Could he have left the church on his own?"

"Yes, it's possible."

"Then we need to do a careful check of the places he could have walked to before succumbing to the poison."

"I called the station as soon as I realized what we had. I sent my own people to check around the church for more of the beans and to be on the lookout for Cheevers. Sergeant Shwinnard has assigned police to scour the area around the church and the village."

"You took a sample of Erlich's blood. Did you find any of this poison in his system?"

"No, just the sedative."

"Cheevers was seen saying the rosary that night. If this bead had fallen off because the rosary was broken, I think your team would have found others. Maybe this was separate from the rosary which he still might be carrying around with him."

"I've done some research and about six years ago there was an alert by retailers to return bracelets made in Peru and sold by the Eden Project in St. Austel, Cornwall. Some of those bracelets could still be out there."

"I can't believe this poison bean was made into jewelry. What if a child gets hold of it?"

"There is no known antidote, so it definitely would be fatal."

Kara's cell phone rang. She looked at the caller ID. It was Carl Sullivan.

"Hi ... I'm at the forensics lab ... Tell Sergeant Shwinnard I'll be right there." She turned to Harry. "They've found Gilbert Cheevers body."

∽

Her friends were keeping watch over Darlene. Right now it was the changing of the guard. Cheryl was leaving and Minnie came by to take over. They sat around the living room knitting and talking quietly. Darlene hadn't added a row in her scarf for the past hour. She kept glancing out the window.

"I have to get going but I'll be back tonight. I'm making a casserole for us." Cheryl put her fingerless mittens in the knitting basket and hugged her friend before leaving. Minnie went out to the kitchen and returned with a mug which she gave to Darlene. Her hand shook and spilled coffee on her bathrobe. Minnie used a napkin to dab at the stain.

"I can't sleep but I feel like I'm half awake, walking around like a zombie. Where do you think he could be?"

"We've helped you search the house and the neighborhood. The police have been all over the church and the village. Do you think he could have left town?"

"How? He didn't have a car and he never went beyond the borders of the village. The furthest he ever goes is to the Wakefield Riverfires on Thursday nights in the summer, and that's less than a mile away."

"Maybe he went off with a friend?"

"You mean like another woman?" Darlene was irate.

"No, no. I meant like a buddy. Someone he hangs around with."

"He wasn't very social. I'm his best buddy. He liked to stop in at the stores in Peace Dale and chat with the help."

"So, you don't know of any new person he may be spending time with?"

"No. I think he would have said something. But then, he's been pretty mad with me since I let the cat out of the bag about his little hobby."

"Strange choice of hobby - listening in on confessions. My Maxwell likes to make things. He carves all sorts of stuff. He brought home a bunch of wooden Easter eggs this weekend. I'm thinking of having a yard sale when I know he's going to be gone for the day. I could make a bundle on all the junk he brings home."

Darlene wasn't paying attention. She jumped up. Two cars had parked in the front of her house. "Sergeant Shwinnard is here with a woman. Maybe they have some news?" She rushed to the front door to let them in. She stood waiting for them to explain why they were there, knowing the reason without anything being said.

"Have you found Gilbert? Have you found my husband?"

The Sergeant led her to the chair. "Mrs. Cheevers, this is Detective Langley."

Kara spoke gently to her. "We believe we've found someone matching the photo you provided for the sergeant."

"He's dead, isn't he?" She tried to stand for a moment, but her knees were weak.

"We'd like you to make a positive identification if you feel you're able."

"I think I can do that. I'll need to get dressed first."

"Take your time. Detective Langley will stay here with you and answer any questions you might have. She'll drive you to the morgue when you're ready. I have to get back to the station but call me if there's anything I can do for you, Mrs. Cheevers."

She watched as he left, then commented, "Such a lovely man. Minnie, could you go up to my room and pick out an outfit for me, please?"

When they were alone, Darlene looked at Kara. "Where did you find his body?"

"He was in Riverside."

"Riverside Cemetery? What was he doing there?"

"I was hoping you could shed some light on that."

"I have no idea. Do you think someone took him there?"

"We don't know, but he may have wandered into the graveyard by himself."

"When?"

"We believe sometime late Friday night or early Saturday morning."

"He always used the bike route which runs adjacent to the cemetery and he liked to walk on the paths around the river, but never at night. He'd never traipse around a graveyard in the dark. It's much too dangerous. Gilbert didn't take chances. He was an epileptic, you see. He walked through the neighborhood every day. He visited familiar places. Places he knew from when he was a child - when his mother used to walk with him and tell him stories about the historic buildings. He loved them. He'd never walk in the dark where there were no people to help him if he had a problem."

"Did he have many seizures?"

"Not for years. I told you, he was a very cautious man. Wait, are you saying he died of a seizure?"

"We're not sure what he died of yet, Mrs. Cheevers. We'll need an autopsy to give us more information and I'll let you know right away when we find out."

Minnie came to tell Darlene she had put out some clothes for her. "Detective Langley, I can take Darlene to the morgue if you'd like. I'm sure you must want to get back to work. The sooner you have the answers, the better for everyone."

"I don't mind, but thank you for the offer, Mrs… " Kara realized they hadn't been introduced.

"Mrs. Jacques. Minnie."

"Are you any relation to Professor Maxwell Jacques from the URI Engineering Department?"

"Yes, he's my husband. How do you know him?"

"My husband is a professor at the university, too."

"Maxwell is no longer teaching. He's retired and has moved on to hobbies."

At the word hobbies Darlene started to cry softly. "If only Gilbert had other hobbies besides eavesdropping, he'd probably still be alive."

Minnie put her arm around her friend. "You can't be sure of that, Darlene."

"Be sure of what?" Kara asked.

"Darlene thinks Gilbert may have overheard something which could have placed him in danger," Minnie explained.

"What do you think he may have heard, Mrs. Cheevers?"

"He wouldn't tell me all of it but he mentioned a body."

"And where did he hear this?"

"At church. He listens in on confessions."

"Did he give you any idea of the person who was confessing?"

"No, but he kept talking to himself ever since that night. Gilbert was very distracted. Forgetting to do his chores around the house. He kept mumbling about our neighbor's little boy - the child who disappeared six years ago. I think he overheard someone who knows where Anthony Tucker is."

"It would be best to go to the station and give a statement on what you've told me. If you feel up to it, you could do it after I drive you to the morgue. I'll wait here for you until you get dressed."

Kara watched the two women go upstairs and then she called Sullivan. "Carl, there's a definite connection with the Tucker case. Not only do the Cheevers live on the same street, but Gilbert's wife says he'd been talking about the boy after overhearing someone's confession at Saint Bibiana's two weeks ago, the night before Erlich took off. I'm bringing her to the morgue to identify her husband and on to the station to make a statement."

Sergeant Shwinnard met them in the interrogation room. He had the video equipment in place and he helped the women get settled at the table. He left the room and returned with a pitcher of water and two glasses. He started the video with the time, date, and identification of the people in the room, then Kara began the interview.

"Mrs. Cheevers, when was the last time you saw your husband, Gilbert Cheevers?"

"Last Friday morning. Good Friday. At breakfast. He made scrambled eggs and toast for us. It was my birthday." She looked over at the sergeant to confirm this and Shwinnard shook his head, relieved she did not elaborate on her age. "He said he had some errands to run. He must have gone to Patsy's because when I got home, I found a bottle of peppermint schnapps on the table. It's my favorite. He bought me a bottle for my birthday every year. Never fails."

"But you didn't see him when he came in?"

"No, I spent the day with my friends. I told Gilbert I would be back late because Doreen and Cheryl were taking me out to eat at Iggy's Clam Shack. He reminded me he'd made reservations for breakfast the next morning. He always treats me to breakfast the day after my birthday. He called it 'The first day of the rest of my life with you.'"

She began to cry and Kara held her hand. Shwinnard stopped the tape. He left the room and returned with a box of Kleenex which he placed in front of her. "Mrs. Cheevers, you tell me when you're ready to resume your statement."

"Thank you, Sergeant." She blew her nose. "I'm fine. Please continue."

"So, the last time you spoke with your husband was the morning of March 30? And you made plans to go out the next day. Did he seem upset at all to you?"

"Not that morning, although he'd been muttering under his breath more than usual during the past week, as I told you."

"And what was he saying. Were you able to understand him?"

"Yes. He was talking to himself about a body. He thought someone had hidden a body."

"What do you feel led him to think that?"

"The previous Friday night my friends all were busy, so I made myself a TV dinner and took it into the living room. He came home just as I was getting ready to watch my game shows - *Wheel of Fortune* and *Jeopardy*. He said something had started bothering him. He confided in me he'd been in church and overheard a confession. He always saw himself as a good listener."

"And where did he do his listening?"

"At Saint Bibiana's. On Friday night Father Erlich hears confessions from 7-8 PM."

"But you said, he came in before the game shows. Don't they start at 7 PM? Were the confessions heard early that evening?"

"I don't know, but I'm positive he came home before seven because he sat with me that night and answered the questions. It was fun. I was surprised at how many he got right." She grabbed another tissue and wiped her eyes.

"And this body your husband referred to. Did he ever say who he thought it was?"

"He mentioned the little boy who'd disappeared six years ago. He said his name, a few times. Anthony. We knew the Tucker family. I used to spend time with his mother, Marjorie. And Louis, her husband, always made it a point to talk to Gilbert if he was in the yard when he wandered past the house. Nice people. Such a shame."

"Can you remember the exact words your husband used?"

"No, I don't. He was very distracted, as I told you. He spent a lot of time, when he wasn't walking around the village, in the cellar. I showed Sergeant Shwinnard the man cave when he came by." She smiled at the Sergeant who nodded.

"You wouldn't believe how angry he was when he found out I told my friends about his little hobby. But I never said anything to them about what he was mumbling. About the body, I mean."

"What do you remember in regard to the day Anthony disappeared?"

"I slept in that morning, but Gilbert set off early. When I woke up, I went outside to work in the garden. Marjorie called later on to ask if I'd like a cup of coffee. I walked up the street and brought her a cake I'd made. I thought she might like some for the boy when he got home. We chatted and then I returned home before the school bus was to drop off the kids. I told the police I didn't remember Anthony walking by my house as he usually did."

"Did you hear the bus?"

"No, I was in the side yard, away from the road, and I had put the transistor radio on the stoop so I could listen to the radio talk shows. I don't remember hearing the bus. I'm sure Anthony never came by the house."

"Was Gilbert with you?"

"He was going to the library for some talk they were having in the afternoon, so he wasn't home until dinner was on the table. By that time, people were walking through the neighborhood, asking questions, looking for the boy. I told him what was going on."

"Had Gilbert mentioned the boy's disappearance before last week?"

"Not really. Of course the posters were all over the village and so we were reminded of it every day. But he never mentioned it until lately. It began right after Father Erlich suddenly disappeared."

"And you think your husband's death is tied into all of this?"

"I do."

"You said Gilbert was an epileptic. When was his last seizure?"

"I remember it well. It was about ten years ago. We went to a concert at the high school and they were using a strobe light. I could look through our medical records for the exact date because he was taken to the hospital by ambulance. He's been very careful since."

Kara took out her phone and showed Darlene a photo of a bracelet made of rosary peas. "Mrs. Cheevers, have you ever had jewelry which looks like this?"

Darlene looked at it carefully. "No, I don't have a lot of jewelry. Just the few pieces in a box on my bureau. I've never had anything like that."

"I noticed in your curio cabinet you have a collection of rosary beads. Did you have any which looked like the beads in this picture?"

"No, none at all. Is there a reason you're showing me this?"

"We believe Gilbert may have had prayer beads on him which looked like this and if so, there is a substance in them that could have made him sick."

"You think this substance could have killed him?"

"We won't know until the autopsy results are sent to us."

"Then, maybe he wasn't killed. Maybe he just died of natural causes. I wish I'd been with him. He must have been so scared." She began to cry again and Kara motioned for Sergeant Shwinnard to end the taping. He offered to drive her home.

Sullivan was standing outside the room waiting to offer his condolences to Mrs. Cheevers. He and Kara went to his office to discuss the interview.

"I don't think she's hiding anything, do you?"

"I agree. I think she's given us as much information as she knows," Kara said.

"Where do we go from here?"

"There are a few avenues I'd like to pursue. I'll certainly be speaking again with Erlich, Chowdry, and anyone else who was at the school the day Anthony Tucker disappeared. I have a hunch, but I need more information."

"Sergeant Shwinnard and I will continue working to gather evidence on Cheevers' death. Somehow, I don't think it was an accident, but we need to find out how he ended up leaving St. Bibiana's on Friday night and ended up being found behind a grave stone at Riverside Cemetery this morning."

"I'd like to go to the site at some point and retrace Cheevers' steps, myself. Right now, I have some files to go over in my office."

It had been a long day and she was weary. Stewart was waiting for her on the porch when she got home.

"I have a surprise for you. I've been working on it since you left this morning."

"You had me at 'surprise'. Should I guess what it is or are you going to tell me?"

"I'll give you some clues. You're extremely good at figuring out clues."

"Thank you for such a strong vote of confidence. What's the first clue?"

"Smells good."

"Ah, did you cook me a special meal?"

"No. But only because I intended to order a pizza for us tonight topped with everything you love."

"And that's not the surprise?"

"Correct."

"So, if it's not food and it smells good, is it flowers?"

"You're getting close."

"Not flowers, but plants that smell good. Herbs?"

"Yes! Only three guesses! You're amazing!" He gave her a big kiss and grabbed her hand. "Come with me, my dear." He led her into the backyard where he had installed a raised garden next to the patio.

"Oh, Stewart. This is wonderful. She pinched the leaves of one and sniffed. "Lemon."

"Sophia made markers to put next to them so you can teach the baby their botanical names."

She read the marker. "*Melissa*".

"It's the Greek word for bee. It's called bee balm or lemon balm. I can take the leaves and mix them with these other mint plants, pour hot water over them and create an infusion you can drink."

"And what's this one with the tiny daisy flowers?"

"It's chamomile. You love chamomile tea. It's relaxing. And then there's *lavendula* or lavender from the Latin word *lavare*, to wash. A few sprigs under your pillow at night will help you sleep. And you can put it in with your clothes to keep moths away."

She ran her hands over the sage, the borage, and the anise hyssop which gave off a pungent scent of licorice taking her back to her childhood and the penny candy counter at the corner store.

"I recognize this one. It's basil. You use it to make pesto."

"I use common basil for that. This is a special variety called *tulsi* or holy basil. It's sacred to the god Vishnu. In India it's grown in gardens to ward off misfortune." He broke off a leaf and put it in her hand.

"How wonderful."

"I have to tell you, this was all Sophia's idea. She said you told her about the rosary pea and how lethal it was and how you worried about our daughter and all the dangerous things out in the world. And she thought a garden filled with herbs you could share with her in our own back yard would help."

"Brilliant Sophia."

"And Rick and Gino helped me construct the raised bed and brought in the soil and the compost. Ruth did the research on the herbs and I did the planting."

"It's the most thoughtful gift I've ever been given. Thank you for this. I'm sure we'll spend many pleasant days out here this summer." She reached down and broke off a sprig, "Rosemary, for remembrance."

"And I promise you years of fantastic memories. Okay, now let's go inside so you can call everyone to thank them and I can order that pizza."

❧

14

SUNDAY, APRIL 7

The regular Saturday night rehearsal started off with a bang. Literally. Someone turned on the stage lights all at once and a large puff of smoke came from the wires leading to the lighting board.

Molly yelped and then whispered, "That can't be good."

"Where's the lighting person?" Ruth yelled from the darkened wings.

"You gave the tech crew the night off," Clovis reminded her. "Don't touch anything until I turn off the current. I'll see what I can do." Clovis jumped off the stage and ran downstairs to the electrical panel. Rick grabbed a flashlight and followed with Gino.

"Well, while we're waiting, we can run lines with each other." Ruth groped her way to the front of the stage. "Turn on your cell phone flashlights and pair off."

The guys returned from the basement and told Sophia to call the electrician in.

"I think we need to play it safe," Rick advised.

"It's spooky down dare. Great place ta hide a body. All kindsa old stuff stacked up everywaya. It's a hoarder's dream. And you should see dee animal heads hangin up all ova da place. Moose and deeah and I think I saw a bobcat's glassy eyes lookin down at me. I almost peed my pants, Sophia. You couldn't pay me to go back down dare. It's like da bowels a hell."

"It was once used as classrooms back in the old days."

"What did day teach dose kids? Embalming?"

"Maybe you could go out and get us all some coffee?" she suggested. "The electrician will be here in a few minutes."

"Good ideeah. I could use some fresh ayah. I'll get us some donuts, too."

Ruth pulled Rick aside. "Is it that bad?"

"Gino's not exaggerating. It's dark and damp. Boxes and broken furniture everywhere. Condensation from the overhanging pipes is dripping. There are enough cobwebs to make a silk gown. And yes, a taxidermist would have a field day in that cellar. I'm not sure how serious the problem is. We checked the circuit breaker. It doesn't smell like anything is burnt."

"I hate to cancel rehearsal. We only have a few more before opening night."

"Let's wait to see what the electrician tells us. Where is the lighting guy?"

"He told me everything was hooked up and set to go. I gave him and some of the other tech crew the night off. They should be at Wednesday's rehearsal."

"I think you need to call him and let him know what happened."

Kara and Stewart walked in just as someone finished pulling aside the heavy curtains on the windows to let in the last of the evening light.

"Not another snag?" Stewart squinted and looked around

"A minor issue with the wiring. Ruth is calling Maxwell now." Rick pulled him aside. Under his breath he said, "Don't get them started again on this play being cursed. Ruth's been having nightmares as it is."

"You've got to admit, something seems to go wrong each time we have a rehearsal. It doesn't bode well. But on the bright side, I've memorized my lines, Sophia has almost finished my costume, and the set looks great."

"It would be a shame not to be able to do this in front of an audience. Let's hope for the best," Rick said.

It only took a short while for the electrician to find the problem. "You're all set but be careful. I had to fix a wire going to the board, but the main system is fine. I've taken care of this old place since I first set up my business. I'm right around the corner. Call if you need me."

Ruth decided to work on stage, reblocking a scene with Mrs. Boyle and Miss Caswell.

Kara and Clovis sat in the back of the auditorium going over his lines and developing a back story for the character he was playing.

"My take on Christopher Wren is he seems like a poor soul. He tries to be helpful to Mollie. Her husband, Giles, is jealous but the kid's looking for a mother figure not a girlfriend." Clovis opened the script to show Kara the page where Christopher talks about how his life would have been different if his mother had lived to take care of him. They read the scene together. "He's insecure and needy. I see it with the children in our church school. Most of them are pretty confident even though they're little. But there's always one kid who clings to the teacher or has to be given constant encouragement to do even the smallest thing outside his comfort zone. I was like that."

"You were?"

"I was a scared little boy who wanted to run away from everything after my mother died. I used to eat for comfort and I was chubby. It didn't help that the kids picked on me in school. My dad's reaction was to tell me to stop my whining and ignore them. I spent a lot of time alone, reading. Getting the job at St. Bib's helped me to gain confidence; to grow up. I can identify with Christopher. I think this role was made for me."

"How long have you been at the church school?"

"Six years. It was my first job. I was hired the day of my sixteenth birthday."

"Then you were working there when the Tucker child disappeared?"

"Why do you ask? Is it because Erlich disappeared recently?"

"That's part of it. I wasn't a homicide detective at the time, but I was involved with the case. I've been looking over the files to see if there's something we missed."

"Yes, I was an aide. I'm a teacher now. I remember Anthony Tucker. He's hard to forget. Always helping around the classroom and if another child was sad or hurt, Anthony could be found holding his hand telling him everything was going to be okay. He was an old soul."

"Were you there the day he went missing?"

"I've never missed work. I'd only started a few weeks before."

"What happened that day?"

"I remember it was hot and humid and the head teacher, Laura Chowdry, kept the children inside for lunch and afternoon recess. But she did let them play outside for a while later in the day. I remember because I was out in the playground and one of the boys, Jody, was on the swing. He kept going up higher and higher. I heard him shout. 'Anthony, catch me!' Before anyone could stop them, he jumped off and they landed in a heap. Jody was okay, but Anthony had bumped his head. Erlich was on his way into the church and he was furious. He began yelling about ensuring the children were safe when they were at the church and that we should be fired and suddenly he stopped. He was sweating and his hands were shaking. He turned and left us standing there."

"What happened then?"

"We took the kids inside and they both appeared to be fine. Anthony had a small bump on the back of his head. I put an ice pack on it."

"Was he looked at by a nurse?'

"No, he seemed okay. I stayed with him and gave him a glass of water. He was quiet but it was really hot. All the kids were quieter than usual."

"What happened after that?"

"Miss Chowdry and I were getting them ready to go to the bus and a call came from Mrs. Walters that Father Erlich was sick. Miss Chowdry went upstairs to help. He was having a heart attack. They phoned for an ambulance. I took the kids out and gave instructions to the bus driver and finished putting them on the bus. That's the last I saw of Anthony. I often wonder if he's still alive."

Ruth called for Clovis to come to the stage for the next scene leaving Kara to think about what she'd just heard.

Rehearsal went well with no further accidents. Everyone was doing whatever it took to make sure the play would be on schedule and they all agreed to extra rehearsals if that's what was needed. Ruth had a few last-minute notes for the actors before she sent them on their way. Rick and Gino checked to see that everything was locked up for the night. Sophia and Kara gathered up coffee cups and napkins.

"Thanks again for the herb garden. Such a thoughtful idea, Sophia."

"I've been researching about brain stimulation in babies and everything I read encourages parents to provide as many sensory experiences as possible. Smell is the strongest sense to evoke memories. I have copies of the studies in my Baby Langley Binder."

"Baby Langley is going to be one fortunate little girl."

"I know how worried you've been, Kara, but it will be fine. I'm sorry I nagged you about getting back to work. I realize now you needed that leave of absence. You have a tough job and it must be difficult for you reliving those days when the Tucker boy went missing. It seems to have consumed your life right now."

"You're right and that's the problem with this job. It can be all consuming. I want to make sure Carl is ready to take over when I leave. I've decided, after the baby is born, I'm done. I'll continue with the forensics work and the consulting, but I'm handing in my badge."

"This is what you really want?"

"I've had a lot of time to think. Stewart and I have discussed it and we agree this is the best choice. I know I won't be able to leave until I resolve the Tucker case, but I feel I'm getting close to solving it."

"It's been six years. What's happened to make you think that?"

"I had a hunch about Anthony from something Erlich mentioned in passing. He told me he became upset when he'd heard Sean Fenner had been hurt. It apparently brought back a memory of something which happened the day he had the heart attack. I wondered what it was that had triggered his attack and tonight I found out I was right. It wasn't in the files I reviewed, but Anthony was hurt that day. He had a head injury – a possible concussion and now I need to see if his disappearance is tied in to it."

"If the boy had a concussion he would have had to be watched carefully."

"Exactly. But he was apparently put on the bus and no one was ever notified of the accident in all of the confusion surrounding Erlich going to the hospital. I have to talk with the substitute bus driver and to Miss Chowdry. And of course, Father Erlich."

Gino and Rick gave a warning to everyone they were getting ready to turn off the lights and lock the doors. Ruth and Stewart came down from the stage to join the group.

"Does anyone want to go out to eat? I know it's late, but I'd like to take you all out to thank you for helping me with the herb garden today."

Gino jumped in, "It's nevva too late ta eat. Where can we get some calamari and a lobsta at this time a night? I'm stahved!'

"Calamari and lobster it is!"

15

WEDNESDAY, APRIL 11

The medical examiner ruled Gilbert Cheevers' death a homicide. The autopsy confirmed that Gilbert had ingested anbrim. The report stated the poison entered his system from an open gash on his right hand and had come from the poison inside the crushed rosary pea found in the church. The victim suffered a seizure and kidney failure resulting in death at approximately 10:30 PM on Friday, March 30. The report went on to say the body had been moved following death and placed in the graveyard at a later time. The prayer beads were not found on the body.

"If the killer had left him in the church, it could have possibly been ruled accidental. Not to state the obvious, but a dead guy doesn't get up, walk a few blocks, and then roam through a graveyard at midnight," Harry Henderson declared.

"Have you ever dealt with this poison?"

"No, but the plant is common down south. I spoke with a friend of mine who's a doctor in Florida. He said he had treated a woman for the poison but found it wasn't from a local vine. His patient survived. She'd bought a bracelet on the Internet a few years ago. No prayer beads, though. There was a recall. I have the information for you and his number."

"Thanks, Harry. I'll check to see if anyone from Rhode Island ordered jewelry from this company. I'm sure they'd keep track of it, especially if a charge card was used."

"Do you still think this is connected to Cheevers' overhearing someone's confession? I've never known you to jump to conclusions on a case, Kara."

"This is different. It's a small, quiet neighborhood, Harry. Only a few blocks. Yet, a priest, who's directly connected to the Tucker boy, disappears and then a parishioner is murdered in the same church. I need to piece the threads together and I'm sure they'll lead to the missing child."

"And what about his parents? At least they have hope he's still alive. If you find out otherwise, what will that do to them?"

"Louis Tucker has faced the reality his son will never be coming home. Marjorie clings to hope. I've wrestled with this, Harry and I think it would be better for them to know the truth and be able to move on if that's possible. Right now, they're in a state of limbo. It's ruining their marriage. I don't think knowing the truth is the worst unkindness. I hope I'm right."

○~○

A light rain had been falling since Sunday, but the sun had broken through and Kara decided it would be a good time to reconstruct Gilbert Cheevers' final day on earth.

Darlene said the last time she'd seen her husband was when he'd left the house after breakfast on Friday morning. Kara drove to the top of Austin Street. On the crest of the hill was the Tucker House and four houses down from where Anthony had spent the first five years of his life was the Cheevers' house.

She parked the car and stepped out to survey the neighborhood. A mix of homes lined each side of the tarred road. Three simple structures with cement stoops appeared to be remnants of the mill-houses from the village's past. The ranch houses all had a driveway on the right leading to a side door. Some of the bungalows had small porches with evergreens or boxwoods along the front. She turned suddenly at the sound of a screen door slamming and watched as Louis Tucker went into his garage and brought out a ladder which he carried around to the front of the house and placed on the grass. He looked up and seeing her, waved. She was shocked at the change in the man. Grey-haired and stooped, he seemed to be much older than the thirty-five years she knew him to be. He walked slowly to where she stood on the sidewalk.

"Kara, good to see you." He held out his hand and grasped hers, holding on for a few seconds before letting go. "Marge is working in the garden."

"I didn't phone. Actually, I'm in the neighborhood working on the Cheevers' case."

"Yes, Gilbert." Louis looked to the house at the bottom of the street. "I liked the guy. Kind of a loner but he was a good neighbor … I'm sure Marge would love to see you even if it's not expected."

She followed him through the open gate of the stockade fence surrounding the back yard.

"Margie, look who's here."

"Kara, I was just putting mulch around these bushes. I could do with a break. Can I get you a drink? I made a pitcher of fresh lemonade."

"You two sit here and I'll get it." Louis went inside. Marge linked her arm through Kara's and they began to walk around looking at the new spring growth.

"Here you are, ladies," Louis called to them. "Now, I'll be getting back to work."

Marjorie sighed.

"What's wrong?"

"He's decided to put up new gutters and paint the house."

"Sounds like a win-win to me."

"He's had a job offer in Vermont. He wants the place fixed for me if I stay and if I decide to go with him, he wants it ready to put on the market."

"Do you want to leave?"

"I grew up in this village. We made a home here with friends and family. I don't know how I could have made it through the last six years without them. He thinks it's best for us to start over in a new place. Without the memories."

"What will you do?"

"I don't know, Kara. I don't think I can leave as long as Anthony …"

They sat in silence with their drinks. A slight breeze blew the paper napkins on to LuLu's memorial stone. Kara bent down to pick them up and noticed a small, brightly painted egg in the grass nearby. "I hadn't noticed that the last time I was here. Only the carved animals."

"It's new. One of the neighbors must have put it there for Easter."

"Marjorie, where did you get the animals?"

"From the lady who grows the orange roses Anthony loved so much." She poured a glass of lemonade and stood up. "I'm going to check on Louis. I'll be right back."

Kara bent to examine the egg nestled in the grassy nest and took a photo with her phone. She met Marjorie at the gate. "I have to be going. I'm working on the Cheevers' case."

"Yes, I thought so."

"Thanks for the drink."

"Please, come by any time, Kara. It's a comfort to have you here. If you see Darlene, tell her I'll see her later today."

Louis waved to her from the top of his ladder and she drove to the end of the street, turned left, and continued on to the Peace Dale rotary. She parked in front of the Co-operative and walked around to the village stores.

At Pete's Barbershop, she was informed that Gilbert had been in at 10:45. "To get spruced up for Easter. I cut his hair and trimmed his beard. He stayed for a while. It was busy because of the holiday. He sat in the chair and read the magazines for an hour or so."

"Did he say where he was going when he left?"

"He mentioned he had a class at the Guild."

"What kind of class?"

"Didn't say. Gilbert never said much but he loved to listen to some of the old timers when they came in and told stories. Always the same stories, but he didn't seem to care. He was a good listener. I'll miss him."

According to the person stocking new items on the shelves, Gilbert also spent time in the morning at the Jonnycake Center. "He said he was taking his wife out to a fancy restaurant and asked if I'd help him find a tie. He chose a bright yellow one and told me not to waste a bag cuz it fit fine in his coat pocket," the young woman added.

The clerk at Patsy's Liquors remembered Gilbert coming in to buy a bottle of peppermint schnapps.

"What time was that?"

"About 4:15, I'd say. I was sorry to hear he'd died. Sometimes I'd get him to tell us about the old days when this place used to be Patsy's Hall. Patsy's Market was on the first floor and the second floor was rented out for meetings and village gatherings. His parents had their wedding reception upstairs. That's when Patsy Dinonsie owned the place. Pete Cafolla was the village barber and the Jonnycake Center was The Great Atlantic and Pacific Tea Company. I was always happy to see Gilbert. He was a nice old guy."

Kara returned to her car and scanned her notes wondering where he'd been between 11:30 and 4:15. Five hours still unaccounted for during the day. She knew he'd returned home with the liquor. Darlene's statement confirmed this. Kara wondered if he was the one who'd placed the Easter egg in the Tucker's yard. Someone must have seen him during that time.

The sound of laughter filled the spring air. Clovis was kneeling on the ground beside the slide helping a child. "You need to be very careful not to run if your laces are untied. We don't want you to fall and get hurt."

"Yes, Mr. Clovis." The boy ran across the yard to the seesaw.

"Hello, Kara. Can I help you with anything?"

"I'm here to speak with Father Erlich."

"He's usually not here on Wednesday, but Father Lucien's in the office."

"Thanks, Clovis. How are the lines coming along?"

"No problem. Thanks for working with me. Wow, it's too bad about Maxwell's buddy, Gilbert."

"Gilbert Cheevers?"

"Yeah. Maxwell brought him to rehearsal last week to help with the lighting. I guess you didn't see him. Scrawny, quiet, little guy. Grey hair. Goatee."

"I didn't get to meet him. Clovis, how well do you know Maxwell?"

"He's been helping out around the church for years. If you need to talk to him, he lives around the corner on Spring Street. Take the bike path and it's the third house on the right. You can walk from here."

"Thanks."

A woman pushing a jogging stroller passed her as she stood behind the back of Maxwell's house. A young man leaned against the park bench stretching his legs. He smiled at Kara before beginning his run. On the other side of the path, to her left, was Riverside Cemetery. Moss-covered markers stuck out of the muddy hill which sloped down to a narrow dirt roadway. She stepped cautiously around the plots. Some of the stones leaned with age. She gazed over the yellow police tape forming a rectangle in the area around the graves. She observed some of the names carved into the stonework. They represented many of the older families who settled in South Kingstown - Holland, Potter, Babcock, Hazard, Perry, Whitford, Tucker. She photographed the patch of blue forget-me-nots in bloom on a mound above the graves, then moved about placing samples of the soil into evidence bags.

Kara returned to the path. Resting on the bench, she peered into Maxwell Jacques' yard. The pieces were beginning to come together. She stood and walked slowly back to the church.

Father Lucien was testing the sound system. "Good afternoon, Detective Langley." His voice reverberated throughout the Sanctuary. "Ouch! That can give you a nasty shock. It keeps shutting on and off. I thought Minnie had fixed it when she was here on Friday. I heard her whispering a prayer into the microphone and it reverberated loud and clear." He came down from the pulpit and sat next to her in the front pew. "I'm getting things set for the Cheevers' funeral on Friday. How is the case coming along?"

"Actually, that's why I'm here."

"I'll help in any way I can."

"I understand Gilbert may have overheard something during confessions three weeks ago."

"Darlene mentioned it to me when I was with her yesterday. She thinks it has to do with Anthony Tucker's disappearance ... Father Erlich is the one who hears confessions."

"Was he in church much before 7 PM?"

"Father Erlich is not one to make changes in the church's schedule. As far as I know, he arrived only just before confessions at 7."

"Has he said anything to you about that night?"

"No. If you remember, Father went missing the next day. He hasn't spoken to me much since his return."

"Do you think it's possible he knows something he's not telling the police?"

"Something's definitely bothering him. But as I said, he's been keeping to himself. Today is the first time he's left the rectory. He received a call this morning. His sister is dying."

"I'm sorry to hear that. I'll come by to see him on another day. What can you tell me about Maxwell and Minnie Jacques?"

"Minnie attends Mass regularly. Maxwell shows up occasionally and for Christmas Eve service. But he's always available to help if we call him. He's a jack-of-all-trades and can fix anything. It's convenient since he lives so close. I called him about this microphone and left a message on their voice mail. I realized it was his day to teach woodworking at the Guild."

"When did you see him last"

"That would be on Good Friday. He picked up the church's lighting board. We're lending it to the library for a production. We seldom use it anymore."

"Was he alone?"

"I don't know. It was late. I'd locked up the church. He stopped by the rectory to get the extra key to the basement."

"Did he return the key?"

"I told him to leave it on Mrs. Walter's desk when he was done and make sure the door locked after him when he left. I can check to see if it's in the office."

They went into the office and he searched through the drawers. It wasn't there.

"I'll have to ask him about it the next time I see him. Hopefully, he'll come and look at the microphone. It gives off a slight shock when I test it. I'd hate for Father Erlich to touch it – what with his pace maker. I'm sure Maxwell will stop by later. He's always been reliable."

Kara thanked the priest and asked him to give her regards to the pastor and Mrs. Brody.

She drove her car to the Jacques' house and knocked on the front door. No one answered. Walking around to the backyard, she noticed the door to the shed was propped open. She stepped inside and looked around. A counter wrapped around the back and side walls with open shelves above and below the work area. Everything was neat and orderly. A woven basket filled with wooden eggs like the one she'd seen in the Tucker's yard was under the window on the rear wall. Carved animal figures lined the shelves. A chill went through her as she looked out to the cemetery.

She stepped outside, closing the door behind her. The root cellar next to the shed was empty. The garden had been hoed and there was a pile of compost by the wheelbarrow. She scooped a sample of the dark soil into a sample bottle and put it in her pocket. She shot a few more pictures on her phone before returning to ring the front door-bell one last time. A car pulled into the driveway. She thought, at first, the driver was a child, but recognized Minnie when she stepped out.

"Can I help you, Detective?"

"I'm here to see your husband, Mrs. Jacques."

"He's not here. It's Wednesday. He has classes and a rehearsal at the library this evening. I'll tell him you were looking for him when he comes home tonight."

"Mrs. Jacques, when I saw you at Darlene's, you didn't mention your husband was a friend of Gilbert Cheevers."

"He isn't. They've met a few times. He may have attended one of Maxwell's jewelry class at the Guild, but I doubt that counts as a friendship. They had little in common. My husband has a doctorate. He was a professor. I'm sure Gilbert never even graduated from high school."

Kara chose not to react to this small woman's elitist remark. Instead, she took a card from her jacket pocket.

"Please tell Professor Jacques that Detective Lieutenant Langley would like to speak with him and to call me as soon as possible."

Minnie glanced at the card, waiting on the steps until Kara drove away.

A person from the front desk came into Maxwell's class to deliver a message. His wife had called and needed him to come home immediately. He dismissed the class and left.

Minnie met him at the door. "The police were here." She stumbled over the throw rug as she followed him into the living room.

"Have you been drinking, Minerva?"

"Maxwell, did you not hear me? That black lady detective was here, and she wants to talk to you about Gilbert Cheevers. She implied you two were buddies."

He didn't respond.

"Since when were you friends with Gilbert? For that matter, when were you chummy with anybody?"

"I have friends, Minerva."

"Hmphh! I think she'd been snooping around the backyard and the shed."

He hung his coat in the closet. She grabbed his arm and he shook her off.

"Maxwell, have you heard anything I've said?"

"Of course, Minerva. You're hard to ignore."

"Were you buddies with Gilbert?" She clutched his hand. "What could the two of you possibly talk about? He's not even educated."

Maxwell pulled away from her. "I'm tired. I'm going to take a nap."

"Why didn't you tell me?"

He left her at the bottom of the stairs and went to his room, locking the door behind him.

Returning to the schoolyard, Kara watched the children as they were being dismissed. Laura Chowdry made sure they got on the bus safely while Clovis supervised the ones who were being collected by parents. She had some questions for Chowdry and then proceeded on to the Guild, where she was told that Professor Jacques had received a call in the office from his wife and had dismissed class early. She asked to see his classroom. When she left the building, Kara had decided it was time to have a meeting with Sullivan and Shwinnard to decide their next move.

All staff working on the two cases were summoned to the conference room. Captain Lewis sat at the head of the table with Carl and Kara on either side of him. Team members arrived at different times and sat waiting for the meeting to begin. When everyone had settled in, Lewis explained why he'd called them together.

"Detectives Sullivan and Langley have been involved in the Erlich case since the priest's disappearance on March 17. Erlich returned to Saint Bibiana's two weeks later on March 31, the day Gilbert Cheevers went missing. On April 2, Cheevers' body was found in Riverside Cemetery, just a short distance from the church.

"From the beginning of the investigation, Detectives Sullivan and Langley concurred with me on the possibility of a connection to Anthony Tucker's disappearance in July of 2012. Erlich and Cheevers are parishioners of St. Bibiana's in Peace Dale, and the boy attended the church school at the time of his disappearance.

"Detective Sullivan was placed in charge of the Erlich and subsequently the Cheevers' investigation while Detective Langley took responsibility for reexamining the Tucker case. We asked all of you to take time to read the files on Anthony Tucker, as most of you were not directly involved in the investigation at the time. Those who were in charge six years ago, have since retired from the force. When the boy first went missing, Detective Langley acted as liaison with the family and the investigators."

The Captain asked Carl Sullivan to continue.

"Today we've made a decision to combine the teams working on those cases. Evidence has come to light confirming the connections we suspected. We'll be giving you assignments to help in closing both cases. Everyone will work in pairs. Any conversations which may take place in the course of questioning witnesses should be recorded. Any searches must be done with official warrants.

"We've prepared a file for each of you with the evidence we've already gathered and an explanation of what we'll ultimately need to make an arrest. Detective Langley will issue you assigned tasks needed to ensure this is done by the book. At this moment we have two unsolved crimes. Gilbert Cheevers died because he overheard information regarding Anthony Tucker. We have not yet established what happened to the boy. When we have that, we can establish a motive." He distributed the files as Kara looked around the table at the faces of the officers.

She took a deep breath before she spoke. "The disappearance of a child is a cruelty no family should have to endure. This town is made up of small villages with families and friends who share their lives with each other. We all want to know what happened to Anthony Tucker. We all want to bring some sense of peace to his family. I'll be speaking with each of you, explaining what it is we need you to do in the following days to close this case. Make sure you read your file carefully and follow the set protocols and if you have any questions, please contact Detective Sullivan or me before you act. We are obtaining search warrants at this time."

They worked together for the next hour preparing themselves for the job ahead. Kara and Carl sat with each team making sure they knew what their role would be. Officers were given the task of contacting people who were at the school when Anthony attended but were no longer there now. They were to be given summonses. Kara had critical questions to ask them and she intended to do it with everyone present. Three teams with forensic kits were assigned places to search and a list of what they would be looking for. Professor Hill and the forensics department would be helping in collecting and examining evidence. As evening set in, Kara was sure everyone understood what part they would play in solving Gilbert Cheevers' murder and finding Anthony Tucker.

Sergeant Shwinnard and Detective Brown had been keeping a close eye on the Jacques' house. After Maxwell had left the Guild, he went straight home, staying inside until 6:30 when he was seen coming out of the house and getting into his car. Shwinnard called Kara to give her his report and tell her he'd followed the car to the library. Kara was already in the auditorium when Jacques came through the door and stood in front of her.

"You wanted to see me?"

"It can wait." She looked straight into his eyes and he blinked. "Ruth wants to make sure everything is set before dress rehearsal tomorrow. She's asked Samuel to be your assistant now that Gilbert is no longer here."

Maxwell nodded and moved to the lighting board.

Ruth met with the actors and gave them the pages she wanted to review before starting the official tech rehearsal. "Since we must do some of the scenes in darkness, I've asked Mr. Jacques to run through with us tonight. It's hard enough working on stage when you can see what you're doing. Moving around in the dark, if you're not familiar with the set, can be precarious. Heavens knows we don't want any more accidents. All right, let's go to pages 31-33 - the murder scene. Actors on stage, please."

Everyone came to the front of the auditorium to watch. Kara spoke with Rick and they went to the chairs set up directly behind the lighting board. Samuel joined them announcing, "Looks like I've just become the tech assistant." He sat in the chair next to Maxwell. Ruth called for the stage manager to turn out the house lights.

Maxwell, with Samuel's help, followed his script, beginning with full lighting on stage, gradually dimming until the black out at the end of the first act.

Ruth was pleased. "For the first run-through with tech, I think you all did great. Let's take a short break before we start from the beginning and see how far we can get through the play with lighting and sound."

Sophia called out, "Please see me at some time tonight to do final measurements for costumes, especially those actors who have taken over roles. Dress rehearsal is tomorrow night and I want everything perfect."

Maxwell handed his script to Samuel and followed Kara out of the auditorium. "My wife says you came by the house to talk to me about my friend, Gilbert." He took out her card. "I didn't call because I knew I'd see you tonight."

"How well did you know Gilbert Cheevers?"

"I'd been introduced socially but I met him outside Saint Bibiana's the night the priest disappeared. We spent some time together over the next two weeks."

"When did you last see or speak with Mr. Cheevers?"

"He helped me load the sound system in my car on Good Friday."

"That would be Friday, March 30? Do you remember the time?"

"I'm not sure. It was at night. He was supposed to meet me the next night at rehearsal, but, as you are aware, he never showed up."

"He didn't leave with you on Friday?"

"He mentioned spending some time in church. It was the regular night for confessions."

"Weren't you concerned when he wasn't at rehearsal Saturday night?"

"I thought he might be with his wife. He told me it was her birthday. I helped him make a present for her. A rosary."

"We've spoken to Mrs. Cheevers. She told us she was with her friends on Friday. Your wife is one of her friends. Did your wife mention she'd seen Gilbert?"

"Why would Minerva tell me anything that had to do with Gilbert? She didn't have a clue we were friends."

"You know his body was found in Riverside Cemetery."

"Yes, I'm aware of that. Am I to take it that since you were at my house today, you're questioning me in relation to his death? Due to the fact the cemetery abuts the bike path just beyond my back yard."

"We're trying to find out what happened to your friend."

"Gilbert was an epileptic. He wore an alert bracelet, which wouldn't have done him any good if there was no one to help him during a seizure," Maxwell said. "I'm sorry he died alone."

Ruth was calling everyone back to the stage.

"I have things to take care of tomorrow, but I'd like you to come to the station in the next few days to answer questions I have," Kara informed him.

He blinked twice and cleared his throat, "I can be there whenever it's convenient for you, Detective Langley." She looked after him curiously as he returned to the lighting board.

From inside the ticket booth a voice asked, "And what was that about?"

"Sophia, I didn't see you in there."

"Then I'll just pretend I didn't hear. I'm good at being discreet."

"Thank you."

"It's fortunate for you Gino didn't hear anything. He'd take advantage of the situation and make you an offer you couldn't refuse."

"And what might that be?"

"Perhaps his silence as payment for you naming the baby Gina."

"And what is your silence going to cost me?"

"A promise for you to keep yourself safe and not do anything which would put you in harm's way. You're investigating a murder and despite what you would like us all to believe, you're not invincible."

Ruth called the actors back to the stage. "All right, let's do the murder scene again. Are we ready?" The house lights dimmed.

Sophia took her friend's hand. "Promise me, Kara."

"I promise you, Sophia."

❧

16

Thursday, April 12

Gino stood at the ironing board pressing the sleeves of a woman's blouse. Rick finished sewing buttons on Major Metcalf's coat and glanced at his watch. "It feels like we've been at this forever. This is turning into one long night, Bro. And what do you think will happen when they realize opening night is Friday the thirteenth?"

Gino hung the blouse neatly on a hanger and listened to the whirring of the sewing machines coming from the next room. "Well, I'm not gonna be da one ta break da news, dats for shooah. I'll go git us some cold brewskies." He peeked into the study. "You two almost done?"

"Almost," Ruth said.

"Three more costume pieces left and we can quit," his wife assured him. "But that pile will be need to be ironed."

He groaned as he picked up Paravicini's jacket and tried it on. "Fits me perfectly." He looked directly at Ruth before he left the room.

"Was that the evil eye he gave me?"

"Oh yeah it was."

"My guess is he's still not happy about Stewart getting the role of Paravicini."

"I thought he'd be over it by now, but apparently not," Sophia sighed. "He honestly believes the part was written specifically for him. It's worse than the great Santa Claus fiasco last Christmas. He still keeps yelling out *Ho! Ho! Ho!* in his sleep and can't wait until next

Christmas season when he puts the outfit on and becomes Santa once again."

"What do you suggest I do to get back in his good graces?"

"Just make sure you give him the lead in your next production."

"Oh, no. This is the last play I'll ever direct. I don't think I've had a good night's sleep since you talked me into this, Sophia."

"Well, the nightmare is almost over. There's the dress rehearsal tomorrow and three weekends of performances, then we can get back to normal."

"Define normal." Ruth requested.

In the next room they could hear the Gino reciting Paravicini's lines to Rick. The clock on the wall struck one and the little cuckoo came out of his birdhouse to sing.

The orange numbers on the digital clock silently screamed 2 AM. Carl gave up trying to sleep and went into the living room. A million thoughts were surging in his head as he began to realize how important the events of the next few days would be. He and Kara had discussed how many things could go wrong regardless of their careful planning.

"Daddy?" Connor climbed up onto his father's lap and kissed him on the forehead.

"Hello, Buddy? You're up pretty late. Shouldn't you be asleep in your nice warm bed?"

"You, too, Daddy." The little boy laughed. He jumped down and pulled up the cushion of the sofa chair feeling around underneath until he found his secret stash of jellybeans. He brought tiny handfuls to Carl. When he was sure he'd retrieved them all, he returned to the couch and sat sorting them by color.

"What's your favorite?"

"Orange," his son declared.

Carl placed all the orange jellybeans on the arm of the sofa and they counted them out before eating them. The last few the little boy decided to store in his cheeks.

"Now you look like a squirrel," his father said. He put some of the jellybeans in his cheeks and made a face.

"Daddy squirrel," his son laughed.

They counted out the green, and the red, the yellow, the purple and the white and ate them all up. When they were done, Carl took the blanket the boys used for a tent. Snuggling together underneath, they both fell asleep.

❧

Kara awoke with a start and sat up in bed. Stewart turned on the bedside lamp.

"I'm sorry I woke you. I was having a bad dream." He reached for her hand.

"You're freezing. I'm going to make us some tea. Chamomile. I'll be right back."

She heard the grandfather clock in the hall chime three times. It reminded her of a song she'd learned in school. *It was bought on the morn of the day that he was born And was always his treasure and pride But it stopped short, never to go again When the old man died.*

The verses came back to her. "Ninety years without slumbering His life's seconds numbering It stopped, short ..."

"I remember that song. My mother used to sing it to me when I was little," Stewart said as he put the mug in her hand. "This should warm you up."

"Thanks, Honey. I didn't realize I was singing it out loud."

"You should sing more often. You have a beautiful voice."

"Maybe when Ruth directs a musical I can play the lead? Have I told you you're a great Paravicini?"

"Mille grazie, mia cara!"

"Wow, I think you've finally found an accent you can carry off."

"Ruth says I'm too good. My character isn't really supposed to be Italian. Gino's been working with me on it."

"Do you think you'll all be ready for the dress rehearsal?"

"If we don't have any more emergencies, we should be okay. The murder scene went smoothly last night. I hope the audience is surprised at the end. When I first read the script, I never would have guessed the murderer. But you probably knew who it was right from the beginning."

"You overestimate me, my darling. It's not always that easy."

He took a package from the night table drawer. And presented it to her.

"Another present?" Inside was a locket on a silver chain. She opened it to find a small leaf. "Is it *tulsi*?"

"Yes, holy basil to ward off misfortune. I thought you could put the baby's photo on the other side. And in the meantime, it will help keep you safe," he said, draping the necklace over her head.

Sergeant Shwinnard parked at the entrance of the bike path and walked the short distance to the policewoman sitting on the bench. He handed her a thermos of hot coffee and a croissant. "Made 'em myself. You won't find flakier pastry anywhere."

"You're early."

"Didn't get much sleep. Might as well be here."

"Thanks, Sarge." Joanne Carlyle poured herself coffee and ate the croissant in three bites, then stood up to stretch. "Nothing so far. The house has been in darkness since the lights went out around midnight.

"Well, you can go home, now. It's going to be a busy day tomorrow, so try to get a little shut eye."

At that moment, a light came on in one of the upstairs' rooms. It went off a few seconds later. "Looks like someone's awake," Shwinnard commented. He took night vision goggles from the bag on the bench and they both sat waiting to see what would happen next.

The bells in the church tower chimed four o'clock as a figure opened the back door. A flashlight beam flickered across the yard like a firefly and then lit up the inside of the workshop. A minute later, the figure left the shed and returned to the house leaving the yard in darkness.

Kara pulled into the parking lot at the Safety Complex as Carl was getting out of his car. The clock on her dashboard read 5:30. He opened the door for her. "You're early."

"You, too."

"Couldn't sleep. I thought I'd get a start on the day before the others arrive. Nice necklace." He looked at her curiously. Unlike his wife, who loved jewelry of all kinds, Kara was not a woman who wore baubles - her wedding band being the exception.

She touched the locket. "A gift from Stewart. A talisman, you could say."

Inside the station, the day's work had already begun.

"It appears no one else could sleep either," he commented as they looked around the conference room. Officers were busy going through folders, conferring, and taking notes.

Sergeant Carlyle handed them a sheet of paper. "Here's my report on the stakeout. Sergeant Shwinnard relieved me early and is still watching the house."

"Good job. Go home and get some sleep. We'll need you later this afternoon, Sergeant."

Kara read what Carlyle had written, then gave it to Sullivan. He looked it over, "Well, that's a surprise."

"Nothing surprises me anymore," she said, placing the paper in her folder.

Other officers began to give their own reports on what they'd accomplished in the hours since the teams had been briefed on Wednesday. They were preparing to continue with those assignments throughout the day. Phone calls had been placed and appointments had been made with times set up for interviews. Search warrants and summonses were ready if needed. Everyone was well aware of how important this was. There would be no room for error this time.

Final directions were given, and everyone was on the road by seven. The plan was to meet back at the station at four, if all went according to schedule. By 7:35 AM, the room had emptied out.

❧

Carl met Harry Henderson, the medical examiner, at Riverside Cemetery where they oversaw the exhumation. Harry contacted Kara when the team had completed its job. "It's what you expected we'd find. I'll do the autopsy and send the report on to you as soon as I can. A backpack was found in the coffin. It had papers with his name on it and a note to his mother from the teacher saying he'd fallen in the playground and bumped his head. And there was a child's baseball cap – Red Sox. I'll get them to the forensics lab."

Kara was with Marjorie and Louis when the call came. She'd explained what was happening and they'd waited together much like they had six years ago. When the phone rang, she hesitated before answering it. She'd known in her heart what was under the blue forget-me-nots the moment she'd seen the mound behind the gravestones and now her worst fears had been confirmed. She spent the next hour with the Tuckers before walking down the street to the Cheevers' House.

No one answered her knock but the door was slightly ajar. She called in to the kitchen. "Mrs. Cheevers? Darlene? It's Kara Langley." She thought she heard someone inside. No one greeted her, so she called out again and this time heard a voice coming from the cellar. She walked cautiously down the narrow, open staircase. In a recliner in front of a television set, Darlene sat with a rosary in her hand. She was reciting the Hail Mary over and over, very quickly, staring at the beads as if in a trance. She stopped when Kara put a hand on her shoulder.

"Darlene. It's Kara Langley."

"Detective Langley. Do you have information for me? Do you know how Gilbert died?""

"Yes."

"Was it a seizure?"

"We believe it may have been a cause."

"So, it was his epilepsy."

"It wasn't that, Darlene. The seizure was brought on from a poison."

"You're telling me he was murdered?"

"We believe someone purposely made certain the poison went into his system."

"Then it was my fault. If I hadn't said anything about him listening in on confessions, he'd still be alive." She hung her head and sobbed. Kara held her hand. Suddenly Darlene looked up. "I need to pray for his soul." She began reciting the prayer and Kara sat quietly until she had completed the rosary.

"Darlene, who knew about Gilbert's hobby?"

"Only me. He didn't have anyone else to tell. He confided in me, but I thought it was funny and told my friends – Cheryl, Doreen, and Minnie. Later in the week, he began mumbling and talking in his sleep. I told him what I was hearing. That's when he shared with me what he'd heard. At first, he hadn't connected it with the Tucker boy's disappearance, but after he'd thought about it, he realized what the person was confessing to."

"Did he recognize the person's voice?"

"He didn't say, but I'm pretty sure he had some idea. He was nervous and asked me who he should speak to about it. I advised him to go to a priest."

"Do you think he could have confronted the person?"

"I don't know."

"Did you tell anyone else about this?"

"No, I already made the mistake of letting people know he eavesdropped, and I felt bad I had betrayed him. I didn't say a word about what he thought he'd heard."

"Do you think he took your advice and spoke with Father Lucien or Father Erlich?"

"I know he goes to confession every Friday, so maybe he did. I never had a chance to ask him." She laced the beads through her fingers.

"Would you like me to send someone to be with you?"

"My friends are coming by in a little while. They've been helping me with the funeral plans."

"I'll stay here until they come."

"Thank you, Detective Langley. I'd rather be alone. I need to pray for my husband. Gilbert was a good man, but I want to make sure his soul gets to heaven."

Mrs. Brody was setting the table for lunch when Kara stopped by to speak with Father Erlich. "I'll jest be getten him for ye. Take a load off yer feet." She pulled out a chair for Kara. "I'll be settin another place. We're havin a lovely vegetable soup and some of my famous brown bread I jest took outta the oven. Looks like you could use a pick-me-up, my girl."

"Thank you, Mrs. Brody. It smells wonderful."

Father Erlich came into the kitchen to join her. "Hello, Kara. Are you here about the meeting this afternoon? I already received a call from Detective Sullivan."

"No, Father. I came to see how you were. I heard you'd been to visit your sister."

"She died last evening."

"I'm sorry, Father."

The housekeeper served them the soup and bread and returned with a teapot wrapped in frilly gingham cozy. "Let this brew a bit before ye pour yerselves a cuppa."

"Mrs. Brody, aren't you going to have some lunch with us?" Erlich got up to pull out a chair for her. The woman looked surprised and then pleased as she sat down. The priest extended his hands to them to offer a prayer of thankfulness for the food on the table and the people to share it with him.

When the dishes were being cleared, Erlich suggested Kara take a walk to the church office with him. "I haven't been there in days and I have some things that need tending to."

As they went toward the play area, she asked him to tell her about the day he'd been brought to the hospital. The day Anthony Tucker had gone missing.

"It was so hot that day. I'd instructed them not to let the children outside, but when I came from the rectory, they were all in the back playing and two children were in a heap on the ground. One of them was sobbing. The sound of a child crying pulls at my heart. I lost my temper and made everything worse. I could feel my chest tighten and Mrs. Walters called out for help and the next thing I knew I looked up and Effie was standing by my hospital bed. It's difficult to understand how one day can be the best and the worst of your life." They stopped to look at the empty playground.

"Have you made any decisions, Father?"

"I spoke with Father Lucien about taking over for me. The parish will be in good hands. He's a much better priest than I ever was. I'll be meeting with the Bishop next week and informing him of my intentions to leave the priesthood. Effie and Sean are waiting for me to begin our lives together. This Sunday will be my last sermon."

He went inside and Kara made a phone call and then walked down the street to the bike path and up to the Jacques' backyard. The sky was darkening and she could smell rain in the air. The door to the shed was locked. A face appeared in the kitchen window. She waited. Finally, the back door opened and Minnie and Maxwell came slowly down the steps.

"Detective Langley. We didn't hear you knock," Maxwell said.

"Mr. Jacques, would you unlock your workshop for me?"

"Shouldn't you have a warrant?" Minnie challenged her.

Kara took a paper from her jacket pocket and handed it to Maxwell who didn't bother to read it. He unlocked the door and let Kara inside. She looked around the shed, at the counter, the shelves, the photo of Minnie in her front yard tending her rose bushes. She moved in closer to the tools and the carved animals.

"I've seen these animals before. At the Tucker home. Did you know Anthony Tucker?"

"I didn't know the boy. He's the one who disappeared?"

"Can you explain why your carvings are at his house?"

"No, I can't."

"Do you sell them, Mr. Jacques?"

"No, I just make them for my collection." He pointed at the figures. "I've not given any of them away."

"Maybe someone else gave them away?" Minnie suggested.

He looked at his wife and glanced around at the little creatures. "Minerva, have you taken some of my animals?"

"I might have given a couple of them to the children who stop by to look at my roses on the way home from the school."

Maxwell shook his head in disbelief and began organizing the little figures on the shelves.

"How do you know they're his? Surely other people make carved animals," Minnie insisted.

"Your husband uses teak, Mrs. Jacques. It's a hard wood, so not that common. I've had some of my police officers speaking with local craftsmen from Fayerweather House." She took a wooden egg from the basket and held it up to the light.

"You recently finished teaching a class on how to make these?"

"At the Guild."

"Gilbert Cheevers was in your class?" She placed the egg on the shelf next to the photo.

"He attended a session and he painted an egg I'd carved."

"What does Gilbert Cheevers have to do with Maxwell? He hardly knew the man." Minnie was becoming upset.

"Gilbert was my friend." Maxwell placed his hand on his wife's arm to calm her.

"That's utterly ridiculous. Gilbert Cheevers had no friends. He walked around the village every day, muttering to himself. Talking to strangers. He listened in on things that were none of his business. He was a low-life." She threw off her husband's arm and pushed him away from her. He lost his balance, bumping into Kara, pushing her against the bench. He steadied himself. "Calm yourself, Minerva. I'm sorry, Detective. Are you all right?"

Kara placed her hand on her side and winced. "Mr. Jacques, you admit to knowing Mr. Cheevers?"

He repeated, "Gilbert Cheevers was my friend."

"Stop saying that, Maxwell! You'll only make matters worse. We know why you're here." Minnie stepped forward to challenge Kara but at that moment a voice came from outside the shed.

"Maxwell Jacques, we are taking you in to be questioned in regard to the death of Gilbert Cheevers." Sergeant Shwinnard read him his rights. He and Detective Carlyle escorted Maxwell to the police car with Minnie following close behind. A team walked past them on their way to the workshop with evidence kits in their hands. Kara entered the house to help with the search. She moved from room to room. In the study, she looked through each drawer of the desk. When she found what she was looking for, she returned to St. Bibiana's.

All of the staff who had been working at the school the day of Anthony Tucker's disappearance were gathered in the Sanctuary along with two of the students and their mothers. The church school had been dismissed for the day.

Kara took out a summary she'd put together from the statements which were given on the day of Anthony Tucker's disappearance. She intended to read it aloud to the people gathered in the Sanctuary to make sure she had the facts right. She asked those in the room to interrupt her if anything had been incorrectly reported.

"Anthony Tucker was on the bus that day, but he never arrived home. What could have happened to Anthony? We are hoping to find the answer with your help. To that purpose, I have a few questions to ask. Please think carefully before you answer. I realize six years is a long time to have to go back in your mind, but it's crucial we have a clear understanding of what happened." She began reading.

"The bus left the school at 8:40 AM - ten minutes later than usual. The regular driver, Mr. Sherman, had called in sick that morning and a substitute, Miss Robinson, was sent to the church where the bus was parked in the back of the lot." Kara stopped so the two drivers could comment. Both agreed with what she'd said.

"Miss Chowdry gave Miss Robinson a copy of the route to follow. She glanced over the route and followed it correctly until she picked up Anthony and Jody. At that point she made a right turn on to

Austin Street instead of continuing down High Street and turning on to Gould where Jackie Lawrence was waiting with his mom. Mrs. Lawrence, your statement says you drove Jackie to school that morning and complained to Miss Chowdry."

"Yes, and I wanted to make sure he was put on the bus to go home. I didn't want them to assume I would be picking him up after school," Mrs. Lawrence said.

"Is there a reason for this?" Kara asked.

Miss Chowdry explained, "If a student is brought to school in the morning by a parent, the parent needs to check with me to clarify if their child will be going home by bus or if the parent will pick up the child after school. The numbers of children will be different getting off at each stop. The driver keeps a count."

Kara continued, "From my understanding of your statement, the day was oppressively hot and humid, so the children stayed inside for morning recess. Late in the afternoon, before they were sent home for the day, they went outside and played in the shady area of the school-yard. Jody Timpson was on the swing set and called for Anthony to catch him when he jumped off. Is that correct Jody?"

The eleven-year-old looked to his mother who encouraged him to answer. "Yes, Ma'am. He was pushing the swing for me and it got real high. He ran under it and I yelled to him to catch me cuz I was gonna jump. He held up his arms and I jumped off and we both fell down." His mother patted his hand.

"Father Erlich was coming from the rectory to his office in the church and saw the accident. He chastised the aides for not watching the children more carefully. The two boys were taken inside and checked. Anthony had a slight bump on the back of his head and ice was applied. Jody had a small scratch on his knee."

Kara looked at Jody and he nodded his head. "Yes."

"Usually notes are placed in backpacks and calls are made home to report any accidents, but the calls didn't happen because Father Erlich became ill. Mrs. Walters recognized he was having a heart attack and asked for help." She looked to the secretary for clarification.

"That's right. Miss Chowdry had finished taking care of the two boys and was getting ready to put the children on the bus. I needed her to help me. She phoned for an ambulance."

"Miss Chowdry, is that how you remember it?"

"Yes, I told Clovis to give the bus driver instructions and to stress she was to follow the correct route."

"Clovis, did you tell the driver about Jackie?"

"I don't believe I did. I made sure he was on the bus, though. All the children were on the bus when I left to go back inside."

"Miss Robinson, did you know about the extra student? Jackie Lawrence."

"No, I wasn't told of any changes from the morning – except for the route."

"Jody, was Anthony on the bus with you?"

"Yes"

"Did he sit with you?"

Jody thought for a moment. "No, he was tired. I think he was in back somewhere. Jackie sat next to me. We got off the bus together."

"Miss Robinson, did you follow the regular route?"

"Yes, I did. And I remember Anthony getting off the bus. He had red hair and was wearing an orange baseball cap – the Baltimore Orioles. I'm a big fan."

Mrs. Timpson reacted immediately. "Jody, didn't Anthony give you that cap?"

"I told you, Mom, we traded. I gave him my Red Sox cap," the boy explained.

"When did you exchange caps, Jody?" Kara asked.

"That day in school. I wore it home on the bus."

"Miss Robinson, please continue," Kara said.

"I went to each stop and I counted how many students got off every time I opened the door. It was the same as in the morning. Then I returned to the school parking lot."

"Did you check the bus before you left it?"

"Yes, I looked back and there were no children in the seats."

"Did you walk up and down the aisles?"

"I looked in the first few rows."

"But you didn't go to the back of the bus?"

"No, I didn't see anybody back there."

"If a child was lying down, would you have seen him from where you were standing?"

Miss Robinson shook her head. "I don't think I would have if he were way in the back."

It began to dawn on the people in the room what had happened that day. Jody, with his red hair and orange cap, had been mistaken for his friend. Anthony Tucker never got off at his stop. He was asleep on the back seat of the bus when it returned to the church.

"Thank you for your help. Detective Sullivan and I now have a better picture of what happened the day Anthony disappeared." Kara took her notes and went to stand outside by the bus. The rain had not yet begun to fall but the sound of thunder was much closer.

Sullivan joined her. "So, what do you think happened?"

"I believe he woke up and got off the bus at some point and began walking home. He most likely had a concussion and was disoriented."

"So, where would he go from here?"

"His mother sometimes came to school to walk home with him. She told me he liked to stop by a house that had a front yard filled with orange flowers – roses. I think that's where he headed when he left the church. He started to go home but …"

"There are rose bushes in the Jacques' front yard. They're not in bloom yet, but I'm guessing when they bloom, the flowers will be orange."

She nodded.

❧

17

Friday, April 13

Kara and Dr. Hill went through all the evidence which had been gathered from the shed on Thursday. Animals carved from teak; tools; painted eggs; prayer beads made from rosary peas; a photo in a frame. Marjorie had confirmed that it was the Jacques' yard where she and her son would stop by to admire the orange roses on the days when they walked home together from the school. Kara spread out the photos she'd taken in the workshop on Wednesday and they compared them to those taken on Thursday. The beads were not there the day before. Kara could attest to that. She had taken the photos herself. Another finding was that the wood of the boy's coffin matched the teak used for the animals on LuLu's grave.

It was all coming together. Maxwell was being held at the safety complex. Kara would be questioning him once she'd finished at the forensics lab.

"Do you have an idea how the rosary beads ended up in Jacques' shed? They weren't there on Wednesday. Why would anyone put them there, knowing they were evidence?" Hill asked.

"Many times evidence is put in place to frame someone. I'd like to know what you think, Professor."

"I've known suspects who want to get caught. They're tired of hiding what they've done, and they create a situation which leads to their arrest."

"I believe the boy's death was an accident. I'll know better when Harry contacts me with his findings," Kara said as she packed up to leave.

"You're going back to what Cheevers overheard?"

"Yes, he said the confessor was sorry. It was an accident."

"Do you think it was?"

"Not Cheevers' death. I think that was planned. The broken bead found at the church certainly didn't come from the rosary we have here. It's intact. I think the poison was placed into his system on purpose from another source - another bead."

"Any ideas about that?"

"Yes."

"And what about Anthony's death?"

"I believe the boy died as a result of the concussion now that we know what happened at the school. He fell asleep on the bus and must have woken up alone and started to walk home on the same route he often traveled with his mother. It led him to the Jacques' front yard. We're not sure what happened then, but we can assume Maxwell put the boy's body somewhere until he made a coffin and buried Anthony among the graves in the cemetery. I'm hoping Jacques will answer my questions and solve this when I take his statement. I'll get back to you as soon as we've spoken with him. Thanks for all your help on this. Mistakes were made the first time around. We needed to be extra careful this time."

The conference room was filled with officers waiting for news. Sullivan filled the teams in on what was happening and that they had a suspect in the case. He thanked them for all their hard work and assured them he would do everything he could to bring these two cases to a close. He was in his office when Kara arrived. She came in the back door. Reporters were staked out in the parking lot.

"Are you ready to bring him into the interrogation room?" Sullivan asked.

"I'd rather do the questioning in my office. I've asked Leo to set up the camera."

"You look tired. Are you okay? Sergeant Carlyle says you took a hit yesterday. Is that true?"

"I'm fine. I just banged against the counter. I'll make sure I get lots of sleep when this is finally over." She went to her office and sat in one of the chairs in front of her desk. Sergeant Shwinnard brought Maxwell into the room and he sat in the chair next to her. He'd changed into the clothes Minnie had dropped off earlier.

"Professor Jacques, have you been read your rights?"

"Yes."

"Have you retained an attorney?"

"I'll call one if I need one."

"I have some questions which need answers only you can give us. I'll be taping this to ensure we don't get anything wrong. Please be careful with your responses and feel free to interrupt me if there is something you don't understand."

He nodded. Kara gave the date and time and other specifics when the taping started. Then she looked into Maxwell Jacques' eyes.

"Professor Jacques. Did you know the victim, Gilbert Cheevers?"

"Yes."

"When did you meet?"

"We struck up a friendship a month ago outside St. Bibiana's church - the night Father Erlich went missing. He came home and had a drink with me."

"That would be Saturday, March 17?"

"Correct."

"And did you see him again after that night."

"Yes, we became friends over the next few weeks and he came to my workshops at the Guild. He visited my home, too."

"When did you last see Mr. Cheevers?"

"He helped me lift a lighting board into my car on Friday afternoon. Good Friday. March 30th. He said he was going home but would meet up with me later at the library for rehearsal."

"Did you talk about anything else that afternoon?"

"What do you mean?"

"Did he mention anything which might have been bothering him?"

Maxwell hesitated before he stammered out, "No."

"When did you learn of his death?"

Maxwell brushed the palm of his hand over his mouth. "Could I get a glass of water?" He pointed to the pitcher on the side table between them.

Kara poured them both a glass and waited until he was finished drinking.

"Minerva, my wife, told me he'd died. They found his body among the gravestones behind our house. I thought he may have wandered into the cemetery and fell. He was an epileptic. He wore a medical alert bracelet."

"Mr. Jacques. Gilbert Cheevers was poisoned."

"Poisoned? I thought he had an epileptic seizure."

"Did you help your friend make a gift for his wife's birthday?"

"Yes, prayer beads. How did you know that?

"His attack was brought about from a plant called rosary pea. Inside the pea is a poison. It causes nausea and seizures and results in death." She showed him a photo of the peas. "Do you recognize these?"

"My wife threw away a bracelet like that. I took it from the trash and kept the beads. I thought they were pretty."

"Were you aware of a recall on bracelets made from this plant?"

"No. Are you saying I may have inadvertently caused my friend's death?"

"It wasn't an accident, Mr. Jacques. His body was moved into the cemetery after he had died. Probably in your wheelbarrow. Soil samples will confirm this for us."

"I didn't know."

"Mr. Jacques, can you tell us anything about the disappearance of Anthony Tucker?"

He sat as if in a stupor.

"Mr. Jacques, do you have something you'd like to tell us about Anthony Tucker's death?"

He became unresponsive and after awhile, Kara ended the interview and he was taken back to his cell.

It was agreed they would all meet at the library at six. Sophia wanted everything in place before the actors arrived. She gave Gino and Clay check lists for set, lighting, sound, costumes, and props. Ruth was running through the cues with Samuel and Rick, making sure tech changes would go smoothly. They were all in a state of shock when Kara broke the news that Maxwell was now being held in custody in regard to the cases of both Gilbert Cheevers and Anthony Tucker.

"Once again, we had a killer in our midst and none of us even realized it," Ruth said to Rick. "Do we ever truly know the person who's standing next to us?"

"Kara seemed to figure it out pretty quickly," Rick noted.

Gino came up to them with a problem He'd been helping with checking the props list. "Where's da ski poles? Shouldn't dey be just outside the door? Dare not here."

"I used them to reach the top shelf in the storage room," Clay called out.

"Dare in da sella? Down in da bowels a hell?"

"Gino, don't be a drama queen. Go get them out of the cellar and put them where they belong," his wife commanded. He trudged over to the back staircase and stood staring into the darkness below.

Kara was in the front hall setting up the ticket booth when she noticed the top of someone's head barely reaching above the outside of the window. Minnie's eyes peered up at her. "I've come to get my husband's tool box. Do you know where it is?"

"The tech crew stores its equipment in the basement. I'll see if it's there." Minnie followed her down the front staircase leading to the rooms below. She went into a side room and found the steel box opened on the floor. She bent to close it, but Minnie pushed her aside.

"I'll get that. I don't need your help, now, do I? You've caused us enough grief. They wouldn't even let me see him today when I brought him clean clothes."

"I could give him a message for you, if you'd like, Mrs. Jacques."

"You tell him I believe in him. He never would have poisoned anyone."

"And what do you know about the poison, Mrs. Jacques?"

"Nothing."

"That information wasn't released to the public."

"Maxwell told me."

"You haven't spoken with him today, Mrs. Jacques. You should know, we checked with the Eden Project on sales of their bracelets made in Peru. You purchased one over six years ago. A recall was sent to you about the danger if the beans are broken. Your husband was not aware of this. It would appear you were."

"Are you trying to pin something on me? Oh, no, you won't get away with it. I hardly knew Gilbert Cheevers. I was friends with his wife. That's all."

"But I believe it was you he heard in church - in the confessional. You may have been drinking. You may have wanted to get something off your chest." Kara kept prodding her. "What happened the day Anthony Tucker came by your house?"

"I hardly knew the boy. You can't think I had anything to do with his death?"

"But I do, Mrs. Jacques. I think he came to your house and you spoke with him about your roses and he wasn't feeling well. Something happened causing you to panic. I believe your husband will confirm this. He now realizes you may have killed his friend. Eventually we'll convince him he needs to stop protecting you and tell us the truth."

"Maxwell would never turn on me. How dare you suggest he would." Minnie took a knife from the box and held it out menacingly.

"Was that the knife you used to cut the rosary pea? Is that why you've come here for his tool box?"

Minnie moved in closer to Kara until the knife was almost touching her arm. "If you think it is, then there could still be poison on it. You need to move out of my way and let me by." She waved the knife in a small arc and Kara moved back, tripping over a cord on the cement floor.

"Hey, watcha doin? Put dat thing down!" Gino took the ski pole and smashed it on the hand holding the knife. It dropped on Minnie's sandal and cut into her toe. She began screaming, bringing people into the cellar from both staircases.

"Dial 911. Call an ambulance!"

"It's just a liddle nick. Stop bein a drama queen," Gino told her.

Minnie pulled off her sandal and began to groan when she saw the blood.

Gino bent to retrieve the knife.

"Gino, don't touch that. There could be poison on the tip. Sergeant Shwinnard is outside. Someone tell him to come in right now."

"I'm right here. Are you okay, Detective Langley?"

"I need you to take over. Get Mrs. Jacques to the hospital, Sergeant. And tell Detective Sullivan he'll have to do the interrogations without me."

"I've got this. Sergeant Carlyle, you stay here and take care of the evidence." He cuffed Minnie and brought her to the police car, turning on the siren as he raced to get her to the emergency room.

Kara bent over in pain and sat down on the floor. Sophia and Stewart knelt next to her.

"Please tell me she didn't touch you with that knife." Stewart began to check her hands and arms.

"No, the talisman worked fine, Sweetie. I'll be okay, but I think you're going to have to take me to the hospital. I'm having contractions."

Sophia called the doctor to tell him they were bringing Kara in and to have a room ready, then she and Stewart helped Kara to the car.

Gino went to jump into the back seat. "Oh, no you don't. You stay here. Somebody has to stand in for Stewart," his wife said.

"Break a leg, Gino," Stewart called out the window.

He and Ruth and Rick watched as their friends drove away. "Well, dat was a mean thing ta say ta me."

"Gino, he was wishing you good luck. It's a saying actors use."

"I'm gonna need good luck den, cuz in case anybody hasn't noticed," he looked around at the cast and crew standing outside and announced, "it's Friday da thirteenth."

∽

18

SATURDAY, APRIL 14

Sophia made the calls informing everyone their little niece was born a few minutes after midnight and then she went home to rest, telling Stewart she'd be back first thing in the morning.

Kara and Stewart held their daughter until the doctor took her to a special ward for premature babies - to make sure everything was fine. Stewart spent the night in the hospital bed next to Kara and he kept marveling at how perfect their little girl was. When they finally fell asleep, it was almost daylight.

Minnie and Maxwell spent the night locked in separate cells at the police station. In the morning, promptly at nine, Carl Sullivan brought Maxwell into the interrogation room.

"Mr. Jacques. I'll be continuing the questioning begun yesterday."

"Where is Detective Langley?" Maxwell asked.

"She was taken to the hospital last evening after your wife threatened her with a knife."

"Is she going to be all right?"

"Yes."

"Why would Minerva do such a thing? Had she been drinking? She has a problem with liquor, you know. I've tried to convince her not to drink. She doesn't listen to me. But I'm sure she didn't mean to hurt Detective Langley."

"Mr. Jacques, your wife took a knife she believed to have poison on it and could have used it if she hadn't been stopped. She's been arrested for assaulting a police officer. I'm sure you're beginning to realize she's dangerous. You can't keep protecting her. People have been hurt and I think you know more than you've been telling us."

"She didn't mean to hurt anybody. Minerva loves children. We never had any of our own, but she wanted to. You should see her whenever she's with children. Her eyes light up and you can tell they feel comfortable with her."

"Mr. Jacques, what happened to Anthony Tucker?"

It took a long while for Maxwell to answer and when he did, his voice quivered.

"I buried him in the cemetery behind our house. I made a little coffin for him and I planted forget-me-nots on his grave. I visited him almost every day."

"Did you kill him?"

"No! I would never harm a child. It was an accident. He came to our house, to look at the rose bushes and he was acting strange. I thought he might have heat stroke. He wouldn't come into the house so, I went in to get him a glass of water and a wet cloth but when I came out, he was gone. It wasn't until the next day I found his body in my workshop. He must have wandered in to see the animals. Minnie had shown him my carvings and let him pick out the ones he liked sometimes when he stopped by the house on his way home with his mother. Poor little thing."

"Mr. Jacques, you weren't home the day Anthony disappeared. Detective Langley checked. You were in London at a science and engineering consortium with other professors from the university. She remembers, you see, because her husband was at that conference. She checked to make sure. You didn't return until two days later. We found the passport in the desk in your study. You couldn't have seen Anthony the day he went missing. Please tell me the truth so we can close this case. I have two sons and I can't begin to imagine the pain those parents live with. It's been a nightmare for the Tuckers. You owe it to them."

Maxwell hung his head and wept. Sullivan waited.

"My wife spoke with the boy that day. She didn't know he went to the shed. She thought he'd gone on home. And then she found him, and she didn't tell anyone. She was in a panic when I arrived. She begged me to help her." He stopped for a long while before looking up at Sullivan. "And I did. I'm so sorry."

"And what about your friend, Gilbert Cheevers? Can you tell me what happened to him?" Sullivan asked.

"I found out from Minnie that Gilbert had died. She said he'd been found in the cemetery on the child's grave. I asked her how he got there, and she said he must have had a seizure cutting through the graveyard on his way home from the church. I believed her."

"You know now Gilbert was poisoned."

"Yes, I know."

"Did you kill Gilbert Cheevers?"

"No. Gilbert was my friend."

"I'm going to turn on the tape so you can give your official statement. Are you ready to tell the truth?"

"Turn on the tape, please. I'm ready."

Minerva Jacques had called in a lawyer. She was angry and demanding to speak with her husband.

"Mrs. Jacques, you've been arrested for assaulting an officer of the law. Do you understand how serious those charges are?"

She refused to make eye contact with Sullivan and instead turned to her lawyer. "I wouldn't call it assault. She tripped. Pregnant women are clumsy."

"You had a knife in your hand. A knife you thought had a deadly poison on the tip. You pointed it at Detective Langley. There were witnesses."

"It didn't have poison on it, because if it did, I wouldn't be here now, would I? I should be suing that guy who hit me with the ski pole." She looked at her lawyer expecting him to agree with her. He leaned over to caution her not to say anymore but she had no intention of taking advice from him.

Sullivan continued. "Mrs. Jacques, how did you know about the poison?"

"From my husband, of course. He bought me a bracelet made of rosary peas and there was a recall. He was supposed to send it back, but he kept it."

"Why would he keep it?"

"He's old and forgetful."

"Why would he use the poison to kill his friend, Gilbert Cheevers?"

"I've told you, Gilbert was not his friend. He threatened Maxwell because he'd overheard him in the confessional."

"Do you have any idea what your husband told the priest in the confessional, Mrs. Jacques?"

"To be clear, the priest wasn't even in the confessional. Maxwell only wanted to get it off his conscience that he'd buried the Tucker child."

"How did the boy die? Did your husband tell you?" Sullivan wondered what her story would be.

"Maxwell tells me everything. He said Anthony had been in his workshop and seemed to have sunstroke. He went into the house to get the boy a drink of water and when he came back out, Anthony was dead. My husband is not a brave man. He was afraid he'd be held responsible and so he buried him."

"And Gilbert overheard him in church saying he buried Anthony Tucker?"

"Yes. Gilbert confronted him and Maxwell had to do something about it. He knew Gilbert liked to drink the whiskey Father Erlich kept in his medicine cabinet, so he drugged him, put the poison on his wound, and led him out to the car. Gilbert died on the way home. Maxwell realized he'd left the rosary in the office and when he went back to get it, Father Erlich was there sleeping at his desk with the whiskey next to him. He led the priest out to the confessional and then came home and dumped the body in the graveyard. I'm sure my husband will give you the exact same story."

"We've spoken to him and he's given his statement," Sullivan informed her.

"There, you see. He admitted to all of it."

"Actually, his was a bit different from yours. There are a few details we need to straighten out before we charge him."

"Maybe I can help you with those? And you could drop the assault charges?" Minnie suggested.

"You were observed going into your husband's workshop early on Friday."

"That's ridiculous. Who could see me in the pitch dark?"

"So, you admit going out to the shed. Why did you go to the shed at 3 AM, Mrs. Jacques?" She looked at her lawyer who advised her not to answer.

"Perhaps you could help us with one other detail?"

"I'll try." She was becoming a bit more compliant.

"You were at the church Friday, fixing the sound system. Gilbert was there, too. Is that when he recognized your voice? Did he hear you saying a prayer into the microphone? Did he confront you? You knew he would be back that night to go to confession. Were you waiting for him, Mrs. Jacques? Waiting to poison him?"

She sat rigid, refusing to look at Sullivan who took out Maxwell's passport and put it on the table. "Do you recognize this?"

Minnie opened it up. "It's my husband's passport."

"Yes, it is. You said your husband was in his workshop the day Anthony went missing. But his passport tells us he wasn't even in the country."

Minnie looked to the lawyer who whispered in her ear.

"I have nothing more to say."

19

SUNDAY, APRIL 15

Sullivan gave his wife a kiss and said he was going to take a walk.

"Are you going to the hospital by any chance?" Jess smiled at him.

"I may end up there since it's right around the corner."

"I know you're concerned, but Sophia called to say Kara was doing fine."

"I just want to see for myself."

The two boys were standing in the kitchen doorway. Connor was holding the book Kara had read to them. "Tell her we can't wait to go to the alpaca farm with her and the new baby," Billy said.

"Pacas are Coming!" Connor shouted, waving the book.

"Your Aunt Kara will remember. I've never known her to forget anything important," their father assured them.

Kara was sitting up in a chair reading when Carl arrived.

"I was out for a walk and thought I'd stop by."

"Good timing. Stewart left to get a change of clothes for me and Sophia finally agreed to go home and get some sleep."

"You had everyone scared. I'm glad to see you're okay. How's the baby?"

"Celia's fine. She's in the preemie nursery, but according to everyone nearby, she's quite a howler. I haven't seen that side of her. She's always quiet when I hold her."

"You do have that effect on kids. Jess and the boys send their love and are looking forward to the field trip you've planned."

"What's happening at the station? I'm sorry to drop all of it in your lap."

"Things are beginning to fall in place. You and Professor Hill did a great job with the evidence. There's enough to bring them both to trial."

"But it was Minnie who killed Cheevers. Has she admitted to it?"

"No, she's still blaming Maxwell and she's confident he'll lie for her in the end. She underestimates how angry he is that she killed his friend."

"I don't think she was aware he and Gilbert had been spending time together."

"Maxwell admits to helping her bury the boy. But she was still sure we'd believe her version of the story until I took out the passport proving Maxwell was out of the country and couldn't have been responsible for Anthony's death."

"It seems like you're building a strong case."

"We're still piecing together what happened between Minnie and Gilbert. He obviously didn't know it was Minnie in the confessional that night. When he finally realized it, he must have confronted her in the church. She knew he'd be there Friday night for confession and he liked to drink Father Erlich's whiskey, so she drugged it. It made it easier for her to use the knife to get the poison into his system through the gash in his hand. The mallet from Maxwell's workshop tested positive for traces of anbrim. She'd smashed some of the beads to make a paste with the inside of the rosary pea."

"Those beads have an extremely hard shell but it's the inside that is toxic. Maxwell wasn't aware of this but Minnie let it slip she was. Did you find out how Father Erlich became involved that night?"

"She had to return to the office later for the rosary beads when she realized she'd left them behind and that's when she found Erlich. He'd drunk the rest of the drugged whiskey from the bottle and was disoriented – almost unconscious. She led the priest to the confessional and left him there. Gilbert was already dead in the back seat of the car. I think she intended for Maxwell to take care of the body as he'd done before, but changed her mind and took matters into her own hands. She put Gilbert in the wheelbarrow and dumped him in the graveyard. Professor Hill's trace analysis determined the soil samples at the grave and on Gilbert's clothes were from the compost pile in the Jacques' backyard. Fibers from his sweater were found in the car."

"It was the flowers which made me suspect both Minnie and Maxwell were involved." Kara said. "When I saw the forget-me-nots, I knew someone was carrying a lot of guilt. How are the Tuckers?"

"Father Erlich has been with them. The memorial service will be private - as soon as Harry's report is complete and the boy can be laid to rest again."

A nurse came in and Carl got up to leave. "I don't know how I'm going to do this job without you."

"You did great. You're more than ready and you have so many bright people around you."

He turned to go and heard her say in her best Lauren Bacall voice, "And if you ever need me, all you have to do is whistle."

"That was a terrible impression," he laughed.

"I guess it runs in the family."

∽

She awoke later in the day, to find Father Erlich sitting by her bed.

"Is this an official visit? Because if it is, I have to confess, I'm not Catholic."

"Mrs. Brody was worried about you. She sent me with a loaf of her brown bread." He pointed to the package on her side table.

"I heard you've been spending time with the Tuckers. I intend to see them as soon as I'm out of the hospital."

"They know you've been thinking of them and wanted me to tell you how grateful they are for all you've done."

"I wish it would have ended differently."

"We all do. So many years not knowing. Putting life on hold. Waiting."

"And how are you, Father?"

"I'll be fine. Effie and I will be getting married as soon as we know you can be at the ceremony. I said my last sermon this morning. Matthew 10:13 –15. The one I was preparing the day I disappeared."

"Suffer the Little Children," she said.

"… for of such is the kingdom of heaven." He took her hand and kissed it. "And now I'm going to see that little girl of yours and give her a special blessing. Have you chosen a name?"

"Celia Antonia Langley," Kara answered with a smile.

∾

"Sophia, when can we git to see little Gina?"

"Gino, that isn't the name Kara and Stewart have chosen. She's been named after Kara's sister, Celia."

"Well, dats pretty ungrateful. I saved her life, ya know?"

Ruth and Rick sighed.

"Yes, we all know, Gino. You'll never let us forget it."

"She coulda been poisoned. Dat knife was pointed straight at her."

"Gino, the knife didn't have poison on it. The one Minnie used to pry open the rosary pea and cut Gilbert with was found in Maxwell's workshop."

"Dat dame thought it was poison."

"She was wrong, but that still doesn't take away from how brave you were. You didn't know and still you jumped right in," Ruth said.

"Please, don't encourage him. His ego is bursting at the seams as it is. Everyone is congratulating him on his brilliant acting debut."

"He was pretty good, you have to admit," Rick said.

"Tanks, Bro. I can always count on you to have my back. Now when can we go see my new goddaughter?"

∾

MAY

Our birth is but a sleep
and a forgetting
The soul that rises with us
our life's star
Hath had elsewhere its setting
And cometh from afar
from "Ode on Intimations of Immortality"
William Wadsworth

here is the deepest secret nobody knows
(here is the root of the root and the bud of the bud
and the sky of the sky of a tree called life; which grows
higher than soul can hope or mind can hide)
and this is the wonder that's keeping the stars apart

[I carry your heart (I carry it in my heart)]
from [I carry your heart with me (I carry it in)]
e.e. cummings

20

SUNDAY, MAY 13

The azaleas and rhododendrons were in full bloom. Kara and Marjorie pushed the stroller along the grassy path with its violet purples, fuchsia pinks, vanilla whites, and tangerine orange branches reaching out on either side to guide them to the Oriental Outpost Shed. They took turns snapping photos of each other holding the baby.

"Sophia tells me I have to provide lots of visual stimulation for Celia. She has an entire notebook binder on how to encourage neurological growth in babies."

"Somehow, I think you're a natural, Kara. You won't need books, you have instinct. Celia Antonia will be the smartest little girl ever," Marjorie assured her.

"Have you finished packing up the house?"

"Not quite. Another month and we'll be in our new home."

"Is it what you want?"

"What I want is not something I'll ever have again. But this is best for both of us. Louis has already started his job and it will be nice for him to be closer to home. Less travel. More time we can spend together. It's for the best."

"I have something for you. For Mother's Day." Kara reached into the carriage and took out a small box. They sat on a bench and Marjorie opened it.

"A locket. Like yours." On one side was a photo of Anthony and on the other, a *tulsi* leaf.

"To always keep him near and to protect you as you begin again."

The two mothers sat together with quiet memories of times shared in this garden with loved ones. Kara clasped the chain around her friend's neck.

"To carry him close in my heart," Marjorie whispered.

∞

When Kara arrived home, cars were parked all over the street and in her driveway. Inside, the party had already begun. Music was playing and people came rushing into the kitchen to greet her. "Surprise!"

"What's all this?"

"Your baby shower," Ruth said as she took Celia from her mother and began to coo.

Sophia explained, "We'd planned it for last month but you know how that all worked out. So, here we are, all your old friends, celebrating your first Mother's Day with you and Celia Antonia - the most precious little girl in the whole world."

She took Celia from Ruth and began to dance with her. Gino joined them. He sniffed the top of the baby's head. "Ah, I feel ten yeeas youngah," and he waltzed around the room with the two of them.

Stewart traded her a drink for the baby carrier. "Lemon spearmint iced tea. It will revitalize you. How was Marjorie?"

"She seems to be growing comfortable with the thought of moving away and starting over. I gave her the locket. That was a lovely idea, Stewart."

Kara mingled with her company, offering congratulations to Mimi Carnavale and Darren Coleman on their engagement and admiring the diamond when Mimi held out her hand. Suzanne Tetreault brought the guest of honor to a chair where a pile of gifts waited to be unwrapped.

Ruth handed her the presents. "This one's from Vida."

Inside were matching mother-daughter ugly Christmas sweaters. "I intend to have an Ugly Sweater Party this year, so put the third Friday in December on your calendars," Vida informed everyone.

Rosa Brooks joined them and Suzie took out photos of her nephew Buddy. "Look how tall he's grown. He has to bend down going through doorways in the apartment. And he's at the top of his class," his proud aunt bragged. "He'll stop by later. He wants you to know he's available to babysit any time."

Vida brought out her wallet and produced a prom photo of Loralie in a gown on the arm of a young man. The girl blushed when Vida declared, "Not only is she gorgeous, but she's going to be valedictorian this year." She looked to Rosa Brooks, principal of Mercy Brown High School, for confirmation.

"Well, the final exams haven't been taken, but it's a sure thing. We had honors night last week and Loralei not only received the top English award, but she was given a full college scholarship to URI."

"I would never have been able to finish school if Vida hadn't taken me in," Loralei said.

"And she helped me get my GED." Vida gave Loralei a big smile. "Oh, the places we'll go!"

"Speaking of college …." Sophia handed Kara her gift. "I've begun a new loose-leaf binder of helpful information for Celia as she grows up. There's an entire section on getting into the best schools and colleges. I color-coded it for each year. I'm only up to age seventeen, but there's plenty of time."

"Say *thank you* to Auntie Sophia, Celia. We'll just put this right by your crib in case you're ever looking for some late-night reading."

Kara continued opening gifts while everyone took a turn holding her daughter.

Arthur was sitting on the couch with his arm around Lynette. "I could have had this shindig at my place but there's no furniture for anyone to sit on." He gave Samuel and Clay a look which sent them scurrying into the dining room.

"So, when do you two intend to return his furniture?" Ruth inquired.

"As soon as I get my truck back. It's been in the shop for two weeks. I'm getting it tricked out," Samuel said.

"I'm almost afraid to ask what that means," she whispered to Rick.

Toward evening, the party began winding down. Sophia was at the front door thanking everyone for coming at such late notice. Kara went out to the patio where most of the people from work had congregated. They stopped talking when she joined them.

"It's okay. If you want to discuss the case, I don't mind."

"We didn't want to spoil the party with business," Joanne Carlyle explained.

"The file's almost closed now that Minnie has taken responsibility for Cheevers' murder," Shwinnard said.

"And she admitted putting the rosary beads in the shed to frame her husband," Joanne added.

"She and Maxwell are scheduled for trials this fall. We'll all be called in to testify, so it's not over yet."

"For some it will never be over," Sullivan looked at his sons who were listening carefully to Stewart explain each of the herbs in the raised garden. Kara joined them.

"And *tulsi* will protect you from misfortune." He gave them each a leaf of holy basil and tucked one into the pocket of Celia's sweater.

Connor brushed the herbs to release their scents and broke off a silver sprig. He took a whiff and passed it on to Kara.

She held it in her hands saying softly, "That's rosemary – for remembrance."

He smiled up at her and nodded wisely as if he knew exactly what she meant, then bent over to touch the plants. "Stinky garden!" he declared and as if in agreement with his assessment, Celia sneezed.

About Peace Dale

Peace Dale today is a still a quiet little village filled with a vibrant history that is memorialized in the plaques on its stone buildings and arched bridges. It's bound like a Siamese twin to the adjacent village of Wakefield where I first moved when I settled in South County back in 1975. As in my other books, I know their settings very well.

Like the first thespians who produced plays in the auditorium of the Hazard Memorial Building, I spent many happy days staging community theatre productions on that stage. Just as the women of the village took courses at The Guild, I took lessons and even successfully refinished an antique chair in one of those classrooms. All of the beautiful historic buildings are still standing and in use today, and they were a direct result of the vision of four generations of one family – the Hazards.

The history of Peace Dale is closely tied to the story of the Hazard family, who first came to Rhode Island as Narragansett planters in the 1600s. With the abolition of slavery, the plantations declined and the family eventually turned to textile manufacturing resulting in the creation of the village of Peace Dale.

In 1802, when Rowland Gibson Hazard named the village in honor of his wife, Mary Peace, it was comprised of only five houses. The hamlet grew to become a thriving mercantile center with the introduction of carding machines (1802) and power looms (1810) in the woolen mills constructed by the Hazards. They invested not only in their products but also in the people who manufactured them. The 19th and 20th Century mills would not have existed without this family.

On July 18, 1876, the "Narragansett 2" left from Kingston Station to make a 20 mile run on the short line connecting to West Kingston, Wakefield, Peace Dale , and Narragansett Pier. It delivered supplies to the Hazard Textile and accommodated visitors staying at the beach areas during the summers.

Hazard Memorial Hall was constructed of locally quarried granite in 1891 as at tribute to Rowland Gibson Hazard by his sons, Rowland and John. It was the center of Peace Dale's cultural and social activities for more than half a century. Within its walls, classes and meetings were held. From 1940-1954 it housed 100 students, grades 3-8 from Hazard Memorial School. Sewing and cooking classes were given on the second floor until the Neighborhood Guild opened. Today it continues on as the Peace Dale Library with its stone trough (1890) sitting out front, although no longer needed to quench the thirst of the village animals.

The Neighborhood Guild was given to the people of South Kingstown by John Newbold Hazard's wife and children in 1909. It was the first in the United States to be dedicated to the effort of social betterment for the community. Industrial arts classes were offered for women and children. On the top floor, rooms were provided for working women "who had no husbands to support them."

Boarding houses, a grocery store, a kindergarten, a post office, bridges, schools, and a church all became part of the fabric of life to be used by the families who worked for the Hazards.

Caroline Hazard honored her family in the dedication that can be found on the back of the monument, *The Weaver*, which she commissioned tin 1920 to be done by the famed sculptor, Daniel Chester French.

To the Blessed Memory of These Three Men
To the Enrichment of the Life of this
Village Which They Loved
to the Beauty of the Common Task
to the Commonality of Noble spirits
to the Glory of God
Whose Servants They Were and Are

Although her words were written to honor her father and brothers, they also convey the sense of how generations of Hazards, mill owners and philanthropists dedicated their lives to serving their community. This family's far-reaching influence continues today through the Library, The Guild, and the Peace Dale Congregational Church's dedication and efforts to provide service, instruction, and help for the members of this community.

Photos From The Past

The photos on the following pages were taken in the early part of the 20th century by Dexter Hoxie, personal secretary to Rowland Hazard II. They are part of the Photograph Collection at the Hazard Memorial Library in Peace Dale. My thanks to Jessica Wilson, Reference Librarian, for sharing pictures, newspaper articles, and information to help with the background for the historical settings in this book.

Four Generations of Hazards, L-R
Rowland Gibson Hazard II, 1855-1918;
Rowland Hazard III, 1881-1945;
Rowland Gibson Hazard, 1801-1888;
Rowland Hazard, 1829-1898.

Hazard Memorial Building 1902

Narragansett Railroad – Peace Dale Station

Iolanthe Cast and Musicians at
Hazard Memorial Hall

Neighborhood Guild from
Columbia Street

Peace Dale Office Building

Church Street in Winter

Neighborhood Guild Residents, c. 1910, L-R, Grammar School Teacher; Miss Darby, English Teacher; Grammar School Teacher; Miss Lottie Trowbridge, Sewing Teacher; Miss Edith Carpenter, Secretary to R.G. Hazard II; Miss Rose Sherman, Librarian, Peace Dale Library; Miss Elizabeth Trowbridge, Director of Neighborhood Guild; Miss Flint, High School Latin Teacher

Stone Bridge

Peace Dale Congregational Church
The Rose Window

SOURCES FROM THE SOUTH COUNTY HISTORY CENTER AND THE HAZARD MEMORIAL LIBRARY

Bossy, Kathleen and Mary Keane et al, *Lost South Kingstown with a History of Ten of Its Early Villages,* Wakefield pp. 25-34, The Pettaquamscutt Historical Society, Kingston, RI, 2004.

Cotter, Betty J. *Peace Dale,* Charlestown, S.C., Arcadia Publishing, c.1998

Hazard, Carolyn, *The Precious Heritage,* Boston: the Merrymount Press, 1929.

Hoxie, Louise M, *The History of Peace Dale, Rhode Island.* Wakefield Printing Company, 1968 .

State of Rhode Island and Providence Plantations Preliminary Survey Report Town of South Kingstown, Rhode Island. Historical Preservation Commission, Historic and Architectural Resources of South Kingstown, Rhode Island: A Preliminary Report, 1984

Stedman, Oliver H, *A Stroll Through Memory Lane with Oliver Stedman: Stories of South County's Past,* Volumes I-V. Kingston Press, Inc., 1999.

ACKNOWLEDGMENTS

My sincere thanks to all the people who've been helping me bring the characters, settings, and plots of my South County Mystery Series to life: Michael Grossman, the ever-patient publisher; Zach Perry who continues to work with me on cover and map designs; my loyal beta reader and enthusiastic cheerleader, Tracy Heffron; Joyce L. Stevos, Ph.D., who edits my text with impunity and has said on numerous occasions (when I refuse to change something against her advice), "I'm not dying on that hill, Clare!" To the knowledgeable people at the South County History Center for generously sharing resources with me; and Jessica Wilson, Reference Librarian at the South Kingstown Public Library/Peace Dale who provided guidance and photos for this latest Peace Dale Village story. I offer all of them my deep gratitude.

To Charley, my sweet husband and best friend who offers sound advice and sits by me for hours and hours taking care of business while I sign books and talk, and talk, and talk - this wouldn't be so much fun if I didn't have you to share the journey with me.

Finally, to the avid followers of Detective Lieutenant Kara Langley and her friends and loved ones who inhabit the pages of these books, thank you for your continued support, encouragement, and valuable feedback. I couldn't do this successfully without you.

About the Author

Claremary Sweeney is a writer/photographer who uses her vivid imagination to create both children's stories and adult books. On the pages of the South County Series, Sweeney unfolds the intricate plots of her modern murder mysteries and sets them in the local and historical places she knows so well – places she holds close to her heart.

Many of the events in *Last Train to Kingston* occur in the village of Kingston not far from her home, while *Last Rose on the Vine* is set at her alma mater, the University of Rhode Island. The third book of the series, *Last Carol of the Season*, begins on Main Street in Wakefield, and *Last Sermon for a Sinner* is set in the neighboring village of Peace Dale.

Sweeney is presently working on the fifth book of the series, *Last Castle in the Sand*. (Available in the fall of 2020)

Within *A Berkshire Tale* are the original ten ZuZu stories about the adventures of a kitten born in a barn at Tanglewood who enjoys adventures at the many historic/cultural centers in western Massachusetts. Sweeney continues to write other tales in this children's series. Her stories appeal to the young and the young-at-heart.

The author lives in South County with her husband Charley and their two cats ZuZu and Roxie. Roxie hopes, some day, to have a book of her own, but for now spends time complaining about being "Roxie Dammit, aka The Other Cat" in featured posts on Ms. Sweeney's blog: *Around ZuZu's Barn, Conversations With Kindred Spirits* at www.aroundzuzusbarn.com.

Author's web page: https://claremarypsweeney.cardd.co.

Facebook: https://www.facebook.com/cpsweeneyauthor

BOOKS BY CLAREMARY P. SWEENEY

South County Mystery Series featuring Detective Lieutenant Kara Langley:
Last Train to Kingston - 2017
Last Rose on the Vine - 2018
Last Carol of the Season - 2018
Last Sermon for a Sinner - 2019
Last Castle in the Sand (projected release, fall 2020)

The ZuZu Series – set in the Berkshires of Massachusetts, featuring ZuZu, a charming little tabby:
A Berkshire Tale (10 stories) - 2015
The Pacas Are Coming! ZuZu and the Crias - 2016

Carnivore Conundrum – 2017
A whimsical, illustrated verse tale about set at the Roger Williams Park Botanical Center in Cranston, Rhode Island. After a stressful incident with a fly stuck in his digestive juices, Adonis, a tiny pitcher plant decides he is swearing off meat. His mother and the other plants and creatures in the garden explain the conundrum - he is, after all, a carnivorous plant. But Adonis believes he must follow his heart. And so, a solution must be found to keep this baby alive.

Made in the USA
Middletown, DE
15 September 2019